The Butterfly Effect Series book #1

THE GIFT

New York Times Bestseller of Ugly & Mistrust

Margaret McHeyzer

The Butterfly Effect Series book #1

THE GIFT

New York Times Bestseller of Ugly & Mistrust

Margaret McHeyzer

They say the eyes are
a gateway to the soul.
In this case, they certainly are.

PROLOGUE

W HO COULD HAVE known my life would be so drastically altered?

I didn't know. My parents didn't either.

It was a few weeks before my seventeenth birthday when everything changed. I was rushed into the hospital in the back of an ambulance, unconscious.

I got there just in time.

My appendix erupted, causing poison to leak into my blood stream. The doctors operated on me and removed it before the toxins could contaminate my other organs and kill me.

They said I had a brush with death. They said I was lucky.

When I woke I felt . . . *different*. Something inside me had changed.

I knew it from the moment I opened my eyes. Something felt weird.

Something was wrong.

Or maybe something was right.

This is how I received my gift.

. . . Or maybe it's my curse.

CHAPTER 1

"ALEXA, CAN YOU hear me?" Someone pinches my arm, causing me to mumble in pain. "Alexa, wake up." The pain continues and I want to swat at it, but my arms feel weak and weighted. "Alexa," the voice becomes harsher and louder. "Wake up, Alexa."

Shut up! How many times can you say my name?

"Alexa, if you can hear me, you need to wake up."

My eyes flutter open, then quickly close when the bright overhead light blinds me.

"Nice to have you with us, Alexa."

Ugh, shut up with my name already! "What happened?" I ask. My throat is dry and irritated. When I try to open my eyes again, I quickly close them. The light is still too bright.

"What do you remember, Alexa?" the woman asks.

My memory is hazy. I was at home with my parents. I try to remember, but the image in my mind's eye is filled with a white cloud, and only pieces of what happened are clear to me. "Um, I was home." Man, my throat is so scratchy. "I'm thirsty." I try to swallow, but the lack of moisture in my mouth makes it feel like my throat is coated with sandpaper.

"I can't give you anything until the doctor says it's okay."

"Doctor?" I ask as I force my eyes open again, squinting against the bright light. There's a young woman standing beside my bed. She doesn't look too old, maybe in her mid-twenties. Her black hair is tied into a high ponytail, and a bright pink bow frames it. She's got the kindest brown eyes, and a sweet smile. "Where am I?" Looking around, I notice the sterile environment.

"You're in recovery. You came in by ambulance and were rushed into surgery. Do you remember any of that?" Her gentle eyes assess me as she tilts her head, showing me a kind smile.

I shake my head slightly, because I really can't remember more than being at home with my family. "Where's my mom?" Suddenly, panic fills me and I look around frantically.

"Your parents are both outside. They're waiting for you to wake up so they can come in see you."

Although she's gentle and kind, hysteria takes over. My body trembles and my heart rate speeds to an unhealthy fast rhythm inside my chest. "Mom!" I croak through the hoarseness of my painfully dry throat. "Mom!"

"It's okay; both of your parents are right outside. Please, settle down, Alexa." Her gentleness increases as she attempts to calm me.

"I want my mom!" Tears fill my eyes, and my body trembles violently. "MOM!" I yell with all my might.

"What's going on?" Another woman approaches, and judging from her appearance, she's nowhere near as gentle as the first.

"Alexa is panicking slightly and I'm trying to calm her."

The other nurse looks me over and arches her brow. She's older, with a stern face and hard eyes. Her weathered appearance says she's been here for a long time, and knows exactly what she's doing. "Go get her mother," she says in an emotionless voice.

The younger of the two turns and quickly walks out of the room. The scary one stares down at me. My heartbeat stays erratic and she frowns disapprovingly. "You're disturbing the other patients," she says in a tone as cold as her features.

"I just want my mom," I'm panting now, struggling to

breathe.

Her lips purse together into a tight line, and she places a hand to her hip. I quiver even more. She's scaring the shit out of me.

"Sweetheart," I hear Mom's voice, and I instantly relax because I know she's near.

"Mom," I call in a quiet, reedy voice.

She rushes over to the bed and takes me in her arms. I try to lift my arms to hug her, but I can't. They're still so heavy. "What happened?" I ask. The mean woman backs away and disappears, and the kind one joins my Mom.

"We were at home and you doubled over in pain. You fainted and fell to the floor. Don't you remember?" I try hard, but the haze is still there. I shake my head feeling troubled about how I can't recall any of the events that led to me being here. "We had to call an ambulance." She gestures toward the blank wall opposite me. "You're in the hospital."

I nod my head, but the damn cloud is still hanging around. "Why?"

"You had appendicitis. The doctors had to rush you into surgery to remove it."

"What?" I feel a sudden discomfort pinch my lower stomach.

"Your appendix burst and they had to get it out quickly before the toxins spread. You could've turned septic, Alexa." Her eyes tell me she wants to say more, but she chooses not to.

I feel the blood drain out of my face as a rush of air escapes my cracked lips. "How long have I been out?"

"You were in surgery for just under four hours. But you're okay now." Mom leans down and places a kiss on my forehead.

"Okay," I mumble, finally calming down.

"I'm sorry, Mrs Murphy, but you'll have to leave now. Alexa will be in her room within the hour, so you can wait for her there," the kind nurse instructs.

Mom looks hesitantly at the nurse and then to me. "It's okay, Mom; I'll be fine."

"I need to check Alexa's vital signs, then we'll bring her to her room." The nurse smiles.

"Dad and I will wait for you there, okay?" Mom leans down and kisses my forehead again.

I give her a weak smile and watch as she leaves. "Your mom is so sweet," the nurse says.

"Thanks." I take a few deep breaths and shut my eyes tight. When I open them, the nurse is gone, but she soon returns. "What's that?" I ask eyeing the monitor she's wheeling in.

"It measures your blood pressure to make sure you're okay."

"Oh, right."

She sets it up beside me, then untucks the blanket and grabs hold of my hand.

The moment she touches me, my skin tingles with cold. I'm transported to a place I don't recognize, but have no idea where I am. "What's going on?" I breathe.

It's dark and I'm standing outside in a parking lot.

A train speeds past. A light flickers in an overhead street lamp. I turn to my left, and I see a woman walking away from me. There's a pink bow in her raven hair, and a bright red handbag slung over her shoulder.

The parking lot is dark and isolated. I can still hear the speeding train in the distance.

My focus goes back to the woman walking in the night. Her shoulders are high, and she's walking so fast she's almost running.

"Hayley!" I turn to look behind me to see where the male voice has come from. I hear a gunshot and feel the thud beneath my feet. The man is hooded. I can't see his face. He calmly walks toward where I am.

I'm stunned. My voice is stuck in my throat. My hand flies to my mouth in complete shock.

The man looks over his shoulder in my direction, then quickly to the opposite side. His face is clear now. He's young, maybe her age, and he's got an old scar running down his cheek.

He steps forward, and shoots her again in the back. "I told you. You should've listened." He stands over her body for a moment before turning and fleeing.

I look at the body lying face down on the dirty asphalt. Rushing over to her, I try to turn her over. My hands go through her body. I can't touch her. I can't move her. I can't do anything except stand there and watch the rich, red blood seeping from her motionless body.

"Hayley," I gasp.

I'm returned to the present, and she's standing over my bed looking at me with a perplexed expression. "How do you know my name?" she asks and steps back.

Hyperventilating I stare at her. "What just happened?" I ask, freaking out.

"What? I took your pulse." She reaches for my hand again and I pull it back. The moment her fingers touch my bare skin, I'm transported back to the parking lot. The train is coming past, and I see her walking quickly. It's the same. *Exactly the same.*

"Hayley," I hear the same deep voice call.

"No!" I scream and try to launch myself between the guy with the scar and Hayley. But my feet have now melted into the ground, and I can't move. *What the hell is going on?*

The sound of the gun shot vibrates through my head. This time more intensely, because I've already lived this moment.

"Hayley!" I scream as my feet refuse to move from the spot.

Again, I'm transported back to the now. Hayley steps back and her eyes take in my hysterical state. "Are you okay? I'll get the doctor. You blacked out for a few seconds."

"I'm okay." I study her, making sure she's the person I saw in this crazy awake dream I just had.

She steps forward to grab my hand again, but I pull it back, too frightened to touch her in fear of reliving the same moment.

"I have to check more of your vitals, Alexa. If you won't let me, I'm going to have to get the other nurse."

My heart rate spikes as I dread her touch.

My head is jumbled with confusion. I have no idea what's going on. Why on earth am I seeing this tiny snippet of . . . of . . . of . . . I don't know what I'm seeing.

The muscles in my body completely tense. I don't want her to touch me. But she does, and I'm back to the dark lot with the flickering light and the passing train.

It's on repeat. The same thing. Nothing changes.

What's going on?

What am I seeing?

What's happening in my head?

What's happening to me?

Am I going crazy? Am I losing my mind?

CHAPTER 2

I'M IN MY hospital room, with my parents sitting at my bedside telling me everything that led to me being in the hospital. Although they're talking, my mind keeps going to the weird, nightmarish vision of Hayley being shot.

I'm terrified.

I keep seeing that damn vision, and I have no idea what's going on. I want to tell my parents, but I'm afraid they'll think I'm hallucinating.

Maybe that's it. Maybe the anesthetic they gave me is playing havoc with my mind. Maybe the painkillers were so strong that these are the aftereffects of them.

" . . . alive," Dad says while running his hand up and down my arm.

"Huh?" I question, suddenly realizing he's speaking to me.

"The doctor who operated on you said you're lucky to be alive. Your appendix ruptured; and apparently once it does, it can be quite dangerous. It can, in extreme cases, cause death."

"Death?" A heavy sigh escapes past my lips.

"Yes, Lexi, death," Dad confirms.

"But thank goodness we got you here and the doctor operated in time." Mom leans down and kisses my cheek. "We were so worried. So worried." She kisses me again.

"Did the doctor say if anything strange happened to me in

there?"

"No," Dad answers, but looks to Mom slightly. "What do you think could've happened?" his tone becomes wary.

"I don't know." I have no idea what is even happening to me. "Did they give me anything? Or maybe . . . I don't know." Ugh, I'm so frustrated at myself, because I can't tell them what I saw when Hayley touched me.

It's probably nothing.

"What's wrong, sweetheart?" Mom asks as she rubs her hand gently up and down my arm.

"Nothing." I let out another sigh. What can I tell them? They'll think I'm mad.

Dad's brows draw in, and he takes in a deep breath. "I can stay here with her if you want to go home. It's late, and you need to sleep," he says to Mom.

Mom lets out a yawn and rubs her hand across her eyes. "I am tired," she says, yawning again.

"I'll stay with Lexi. You go home." He looks down at his watch. "Take your time and have a good sleep."

"What time is it?" I ask, curiously.

"It's nearly three in the morning."

"You can both go, I'll be fine. You both need sleep." I don't want them to leave, because I'm terrified of what else is going to happen to me.

"No way," Dad says. "I'll stay and your mother can go home to sleep. Go," he says to Mom, who's yawning again, this time adding a stretch.

"I should stay."

"You can barely keep your eyes open. Go home, and come back after you've slept. Lexi and I will be fine here."

"I really should stay." Mom's conflicted. I can tell by the frown etched on her face. She thinks she should stay, but she's tired and needs to go.

"Mom, I'll be fine." *As long as Dad stays with me.* I hate that she's feeling guilty.

"Just go, woman," Dad gently teases her. 'Woman' is his pet name for her. It's what he's always called her, and it always makes Mom smile.

Right on cue, Mom's lips curl up at the corners. "I don't know," she finally adds, still struggling.

"Mom . . ." I drag her title out. "You need to sleep, so please go home."

Her shoulders rise with a deep breath. She lets out yet another yawn. "Only if you're sure." She pointedly looks to me, then Dad.

"We're sure," both Dad and I chorus in unison.

"I'll walk you down and get you in a cab. You're too tired to drive home." Dad stands and makes his way toward the door.

Mom smiles and stands. "Don't be silly, I'll be fine. If you need anything, call me." She bends from the waist and kisses my cheek again. "I'll be back by the time the sun has risen."

"Hopefully I'll be asleep, so no rush," I say.

Mom picks her handbag up and heads toward the door. She stops before her hand even touches the door knob, and she turns, coming to me. "Anything you need, you get your father to call me." She gives Dad a kiss.

Her bloodshot eyes tell me how tired she is, and the dark circles beneath them confirm her exhaustion.

"I'll be fine." *As long as that crazy ass hallucination doesn't come back.*

"Okay." She finally smiles, but it's forced. "Remember." She points her finger to Dad. "Anything happens, call me."

"We will."

The door clicks shut as Mom leaves. Dad waltzes back to the chair beside my bed. He's so tired he looks like he's about to fall asleep, too. "You can go too, if you want," I say. *Please don't go and leave me here with the horror in my head.*

"I'm not going anywhere, except to sleep." Dad slides down in his chair, and folds his arms in front of his chest. "I suggest you try to get some sleep, too." He closes his eyes and tilts his head down toward his chest, falling asleep almost immediately. The snoring that follows is all the proof I need to know Dad's out of it.

I attempt to turn on my side, but the sharp pain in my lower stomach reminds me of the operation I had.

Closing my eyes, I seek sleep, but the recurring images of Hayley being shot by the man with the scar on his cheek won't go away. I huff in frustration as I struggle to push the terrible nightmare down somewhere I can't access it.

As my mind begins to go blank, I hear the door creak open. Opening one eye, I see a nurse standing beside my bed looking down at me. "What's happening?" I mumble as I turn to look at Dad, who's still sleeping heavily.

"Checking on your vitals, sweetie," the older nurse says. "Go back to sleep. You won't even know I'm here."

She grabs my hand to feel for my pulse, and I'm suddenly sucked out of my bed. Standing in a strange living room, I see the nurse sitting in a rocker, and an old guy sitting on a stool in front of her, rubbing her tired feet. "Tonight's shift was hard," she says to the old guy.

"How so, Doris?" he asks while he keeps rubbing her feet.

She lets out a moan and closes her eyes in appreciation.

"We had a girl rushed in with appendicitis, she . . ." The image is ripped away from me, as the nurse takes her hand off me. I stare blankly up at her, and she keeps going about her duties. She touches my hand again, and I'm instantly thrust back in the living room. "Tonight's shift was hard," she says to the guy rubbing her feet.

"How so, Doris?" he asks.

"Why am I here?" I ask them. Neither respond, they just keep talking like I'm not even here.

"We had a girl rushed in with appendicitis, she . . ." The phone rings, and Doris stops talking.

"Can anyone hear me?" I loudly say, hoping the louder

volume of my voice gets their attention.

The nurse looks over her shoulder toward the ringing phone, and her husband stands and walks out of the room. The woman reaches out to grab a mug from the table beside her rocker, blows on it, and takes a sip. I try to walk over to her, but my feet won't move. I look around to find something to pick up and throw at her, but there's nothing within arm's reach.

"That was Jeremy. He said he's coming home for the weekend," the smiling old man says as he re-enters into the living room and sits in front of the nurse.

Her face lights up at the news. "Oh, I'm so happy! Jeremy hasn't been home in such a long time." Her elated expression is enough to make the old man smile.

"You know how he is. He's a New Yorker now, high flier and all that." The old man chuckles. "You were telling me about today."

I'm forced back into the present as the nurse releases my arm and moves to grab the chart from the foot of my bed to write something down. I stare at her, wondering how she's remaining so calm while my heart beats so forcefully that I can hear it loudly pounding in my ears. How did she not see that?

"Do you need to go to the bathroom?" she asks me in a hushed tone.

I look over to Dad, who's now snoring even louder. I shake my head at her. I'm too terrified to open my mouth and say anything, because whatever happened seems one-sided. I'm part of her world, but she's not a part of mine.

What a damn nightmare.

"I'll be back in when the doctor makes his rounds in the morning. Okay?" I nod my head, but inside I'm still freaking out. "If you need anything, press the buzzer and one of us will come in." She places the buzzer beside me, and I nod my head again. "Goodnight, sugar."

"'Night," I say in a small voice.

She leaves my room, and I'm left with only my own thoughts,

and absolutely terrifying images of what's happening inside my head.

I clasp my eyes tightly shut and try to ignore the videos playing in my mind. I'll try to get some sleep, and when I wake in the morning, hopefully all this crap going on will be gone, nothing more than a temporary glitch with my head. A drug-induced malfunction.

Yep, that's got to be it.

I was given something that didn't agree with me, and it's making me hallucinate. It's got to be that, just a stupid hallucination. *Damned drugs.*

In an effort to turn, I once again feel the stabbing pain in my side. Damn it, I can't even get comfortable.

I finally manage to close my eyes, and find solace in the dark . . . *for now.*

CHAPTER 3

"ALEXA, WAKE UP," a gentle voice rouses me from my sleep.

"Huh?" I mumble as I bring my hand up to run over my face.

"Wake up."

I look for Dad, but he's no longer in the room. The sun breaking in through the window tells me it's early morning, and the raw ache in my side immediately reminds me where I am.

"Where's Dad?" I ask the woman standing beside my bed.

"He stepped out to get a coffee." I try to sit up in bed, but wince in pain as a shard of what feels like glass stabs me in my side. "Don't try to get up yet."

I lay back down, and take in the appearance of the nurse. She has the darkest eyes I've ever seen and her long black hair is pulled back into a severe ponytail. She has square framed glasses, and her face is impeccably made up. She's youngish, maybe mid-thirties.

"How are you feeling?" she asks while she looks down at her watch.

I have a strong feeling she's not really interested in the answer, more like making small talk. How weird. "I'm okay." Her eyes dart to the door, then back to me. She plasters a fake smile on her face and looks at her watch again. "Are you waiting for someone?" My eyes move to the door then back to her.

"Dr. Smith, who performed the operation, will be in very soon." Her eyebrows tighten close together, and the fake smile stiffens even further.

Something's not quite right.

My gaze inconspicuously drags down her body. She's wearing a hospital uniform and looks like everyone else I've seen. Nothing seems out of place, but then again, the operation and hallucinations have exhausted me.

The door opens, and an older man walks in carrying a clipboard. He's got a white doctor's coat on, and a stethoscope around his neck. He's quite fit for his age, his upper body bulk a dead giveaway that he spends a lot of time in the gym. Beneath his doctor's coat, I can see hints of the designer suit hugging his body perfectly. His thick, dark hair is impeccably combed to the side, and his face has a full, manicured beard. "Alexa, how are you feeling this morning?" he asks as he stops beside the bed.

"Okay." I don't offer him anything else. There's something really off about this entire situation. I can't quite place it, but something is . . . *weird.*

"Can I have a look at your incision?"

"You operated on me?" I'm eager to know if anything happened during surgery, but I don't dare raise the question. Something about these two has me feeling very uneasy. My stomach roils with nerves and my skin pebbles with anxiety.

"I did. You were unconscious when you arrived."

"I was?" I stare at his coat and notice that neither he nor the nurse have name badges. Maybe I watch too much TV, but I thought all hospital staff wore them.

"You were. Your appendix had ruptured on the way here. So your timeframe for recovery is slightly different, as was your operation."

My operation was different. "How was it different, Doctor . . ." I pause and wait for his name.

"Smith. Dr. Smith." He takes a breath and starts telling me about the operation. "Because it had ruptured, it means we had to do open surgery and where the incision is, there's packing around it."

I shake my head and scrunch my mouth at him. "I have no idea what you're talking about," I say, still confused by the description. I'm clueless, but it just sounds icky.

"First, you need to take a course of antibiotics to make sure you don't develop an infection."

"Okay." I blink and hold my hand up to the doctor to stop him talking. "Can you wait for my Dad to come back? He'll understand all this better."

"I'm on my rounds, so I'll come back later. I just want to see how the wound is healing. May I?" He takes a pair of surgical gloves out of his pocket and puts them on, and the nurse does the same thing.

"Um, yeah, sure."

The nurse pulls down the blanket, and Dr. Smith moves my clothes and takes the bandage off to look. "It's healing nicely. The packing around the wound needs to be changed, and you need to keep the area dry. Now, tell me something." He takes his gloves off and steps back. "How are you feeling?"

"Sore," I automatically reply.

"Is that all?"

The question is innocent enough, but the hard tone behind his words tells me he's asking something much more involved. "What do you mean?" I finally answer, trying to formulate the words in my mind before I tell him about my bizarre hallucinations.

"Are you feeling dizzy, or seeing black dots or maybe hearing things?"

"Hearing things?" I say way too eagerly. "Like what?" Hell, I'm not telling him anything. I'm shutting my mouth.

He shrugs casually, but his cold eyes stay glued to me. "Anything. Anything at all." It sounds like he's fishing for answers.

My brain tells me to not say anything. And I like listening to my brain; it's usually right. "Nah." I shake my head at him.

He steps closer to the bed, and reaches for my hand. "If there's anything we can do for you." As soon as his skin connects with mine I'm swept away.

I'm in a car with him and his nurse. There's no conversation between them, just complete quiet. And as quickly as I was sitting in his car, I'm back in the hospital room.

I look to him, and notice his eyes are wide as he gives a small nod to the nurse.

"Okay," I say trying to sound normal, like nothing happened.

"I'll be in touch, Alexa." He looks to the nurse and nods again, they both turn to leave.

The door closes behind them, and I let out a ragged breath. *What's going on?* Truth be told, I have no idea and I'm scared to death.

Within a few minutes, Dad enters the room carrying a paper coffee cup and a brown paper bag. "You're awake?" he asks in surprise. "Your mother is on her way back. She wanted to be here when the doctor comes in to see you."

"They just left." I gesture toward the door. "You probably passed him and his nurse in the hall."

"I think we missed each other, because the only doctor I saw wasn't the one who talked to your mother and me after surgery."

"Okay," I say again. None of this makes any sense.

The smell of something delicious wafts through the room the moment Dad opens the paper bag. As he eats it, my stomach growls with hunger. "So, what did the doctor say?" He takes a bite and my stomach grumbles again.

"He was saying something about packing the wound, I really don't know, I kinda wasn't listening."

"Lexi, this is about your health." He pointedly looks at me.

I know, but I can't tell him I'm freaking out because something's going on with my head. "Sorry, Dad, I'm still kinda . . . hazy, you know?" Dad nods and shoves the last bite into his mouth. "Can you do something for me?"

"What do you need?" he walks over to the small trash can in my room, and throws out the empty brown bag.

"Can you hold my hand, please?"

"Um, sure." Dad takes a seat beside me, and grabs onto my hand. He gently rubs his thumb over the tender skin. I feel . . . nothing.

I squint at his hand and make sure he's actually touching me. And he is, but I'm getting no image, no hallucination . . . nothing. "You okay?" he asks with worry.

"Yeah, I'm great. I'm just sore." *And completely weirded out.*

"Hey, here's my girl." Mom opens the door, and enters my room. She's still got dark circles beneath her eyes, but at least she's looking a lot more like Mom than she did last night. She leans down and gives me a kiss on the cheek, then gives Dad a kiss too.

No hallucination.

"I just saw Dr. Smith and he said he'll be in to check you out in a few minutes."

"Dr. Smith, the guy who was just in here?" I look between my parents in question.

"The doctor who operated on you."

"Okay." Man, how annoying, it seems that's all I can say. But, at least when he comes in he can tell my parents what he was telling me and hopefully all this will make sense. Maybe the drugs they gave me have side effects, and my side effect is *hallucinations.*

My mom had to have her tonsils out a couple of years ago, and they gave her these really strong pain killers to help her through the first few days after the surgery. Mom said they were so strong they were causing her to see things. So, I bet they pumped my body with heaps of those pain killers, which is why I'm seeing things.

Yeah, that's got to be it.

Mom starts telling us something when the door opens, and a

man and a young nurse enter. "Hi there, Alexa. I was the doctor who operated on you yesterday. How are you feeling?"

What the hell is happening? I dart my eyes to the four other people in the room, and bring my hand up to scratch my head. "Who are you?"

"Dr. Smith, and this is one of the nurses who assisted me, Katie."

"Hi," she warmly says and steps forward.

"You're not Dr. Smith," I say as I try to readjust myself in the bed. But the biting pain in my side prevents me from moving too much.

"Yes, he is," Mom says coming to stand beside my bed.

"Yeah, he's the one who operated," Dad adds.

My brows scrunch together, and I notice the obvious differences between this Dr. Smith, and the one who was in here not even half an hour ago. "Are there two Dr. Smiths?"

"There are two more in this hospital. But neither of them are working this week." Dr. Smith steps forward, worry carved on his face. "Are you okay, Alexa? You've gone quite pale." He sweeps his hand to my forehead and I'm sucked away from this room into a broom closet. Dr. Smith and his very pretty nurse are in there together 'enjoying' each other's company. He's devouring her mouth while his hands are all over her breasts. He growls and she lets out a breathy moan.

"Oh God," I say to myself and try to look away from the illicit tryst going on in the broom closet.

I'm torn away from the torrid scene between the doctor and nurse when Dr. Smith removes his hand. *Thank God.* I'm transported back to my hospital room, where Dr. Smith is now standing a foot from my bed.

My hands begin to shake and my palms sweat as I keep an eye on the doctor and his nurse. "Would either of the other two doctors have come in this morning?" I ask, trying to keep my voice steady so I don't give anything away.

"I doubt it, both are out of town." Dr. Smith draws his brows together. "What's happening, Alexa?"

The concern in the room is all focused on me. The doctor looks worried, and even though his nurse has said nothing since she's been in here, the look on her face screams volumes.

She thinks I'm losing my mind. Maybe I am.

"Didn't you say the doctor already came in and was going to come back to talk to us?" Dad says, crossing his arms in front of his puffed-out chest.

"Yeah, but the doctor who came in wasn't him." I jerk my thumb toward the young doctor. "It was someone else. I swear he said his name was Dr. Smith." I run my hand through my hair, and the pain in my side pinches at the movement. "Ugh," I groan in discomfort.

"Are you sure they said their name was Smith?" Dr. Smith questions me again.

I have no idea. With the crap going on in my head, I have no idea if I'm imagining it or if it's real. "Maybe I dreamed it." It's the safest option for me. If I insist on it being true, then they may think I've lost my mind.

"Okay, well let's look at my handiwork," the doctor proudly announces.

I cringe, because I know he's going to touch me, but thankfully he grabs a pair of gloves from the dispenser in the room and puts them on.

As I lie back and let him look, feel, prod and touch, I tune out to whatever they're all talking about. I can hear words like, 'aftercare,' 'antibiotics' and 'surgery' being thrown around, but I'm not really listening.

Instead, I replay the dreams I've been having. The ones that seem so real. As a timeline plays in my head, I watch as the other doctor and his nurse talk to me in my room; as they exchange glances and as they leave. The squeaking sound of her shoes on the tiled floor draws me to look at the current nurse's footwear.

She's wearing black, clunky, though comfortable-looking footwear. The other Dr. Smith's nurse was wearing stiletto heels.

How did I not notice them when they were in here?

My brain hurts. My heart is torn because I want to tell them the things I've been seeing. But maybe I've been dreaming them. They're so vivid, so realistic. What is going on with my head?

This is beyond frustrating. I'm afraid to say anything, but at the same time, it's going to drive me crazy if I don't tell someone.

I decide it's best if I say nothing. I'll keep it to myself until whatever this is wears off. I mean, it's got to end soon. I'm probably only seeing and feeling these things because of whatever they gave me while they operated on me, or the pain killers they've given me since.

Yeah, that's it.

It has to be.

CHAPTER 4

I'M GOING HOME today, as long as I can go to the bathroom without difficulty and I can keep my food down. I've been up and walking around since yesterday, but only small trips to the nurse's station and back.

"I'm going for a walk," I say to my Mom.

"I'll come with you." She places her Kindle on my bed, and comes over to help me up.

"I've got to do it myself. You heard what Dr. Smith said, the more I move, the better it is for me." Slowly I swing my legs out of the bed, and drag my butt to the edge of the mattress. Taking a few deep breaths, I stand and find my balance. "I know he said it will get easier, but it doesn't feel like it." I wince as I take a small step forward.

But I can do this. I can make it out.

Shuffling toward the door, Mom rushes ahead and holds it open for me. "You okay?" I nod my head and keep going.

The doctor is right, the more I move, the better it feels. As I walk toward the nurses' station, I see a few nurses huddled together, some with their hands to their mouths, all watching the TV. "Oh, my God," one gasps.

I shuffle faster, and freeze when the television hits my line of sight.

"Oh shit," I mumble. My mouth opens in shock, and my heart

thumps hard inside my chest.

"What is it?" Mom asks and follows my gaze.

On the TV, a reporter is standing in front of police tape. A train whizzes past her in the background. There's something covered in the middle of the car park. An image of a woman is superimposed on the screen beside the reporter. The picture is of a pretty young nurse.

I can't hear what's being said, but there are subtitles down at the bottom of the screen as the reporter tells the world how Hayley Jones, a nurse at the local hospital was found dead. She'd been shot twice and they're considering her murder to be premediated because nothing had been stolen from her.

"Oh shit," I say. Every drop of blood freezes while I continue to watch the report. Goosebumps prickle my skin as my eyes frantically read every word on the screen, and look at the photo simultaneously.

I saw her. I saw her get shot. The guy has a scar on his face and she knew him.

She knew him. She damn well knew him!

My heart's furiously beating, my head is spinning and every word in the English language is stuck behind the barrier in my throat.

Tears sting my eyes, and within seconds they spill over. "Lexi," Mom says as she grabs onto my upper arm. I shake my head at her, unable to say a single word. "Sweetheart." Her tone is brimming with worry. "What's happening?"

The more I look at the TV the more I'm thrust back into the nightmare of seeing her get shot. I could've saved her. I could've said something. I could've done something . . . *anything.*

The turmoil in my head makes the room start to spin. My breathing increases and I feel my heart pounding desperately inside my chest. A huge lump sits at the base of my throat as my stomach flips, then flops, then twists painfully.

Tiny black spots quickly increase in size, and soon, a curtain sheaths my vision, and my legs give out from beneath me.

I should've said something . . . saved her. I saw it, I saw it all. I could've told her and I could've saved her life.

What have I done?

"Guess who's coming home this weekend?"

"Who?"

"Jeremy!"

"He can get time off work?"

"I guess he can." The woman chuckles giddily.

Opening my eyes, I see Doris and another nurse standing over my bed talking to one another while they check my vitals. Not Doris, but the other one goes to feel my hand and I quickly snatch it away.

"Alexa, how are you feeling?" Doris's head snaps at the rapid speed with which I move my hand.

"I'm okay. What happened?" I ask as I look between the two nurses and search out my Mom who jumps to her feet and makes her way over to the side of my bed.

"You passed out. We went for a walk and you passed out. Dr. Smith thinks you're pushing yourself too hard and the pain may have caused you to pass out."

I shake my head and look to Doris. The image of Hayley floods back into my head. Everything about her. "There was a nurse here, Hayley, she was shot?"

"She was such a lovely young girl. Really a beautiful nurse who was all about the patients." She lets out a breathy sigh as her shoulders sink.

"She was shot? Not last night, the night before."

Doris looks to the other nurse with a perplexed look in her eyes. "How do you know that?"

"It was on the news. Did they catch who did it?" The guy with the scar down his face.

"The police are looking into someone," she says. "How did

you know Hayley?" She swallows hard, her piercing eyes looking at me with suspicion.

Shit. I can't tell them what I know. *I* wouldn't believe me. And what do I say? 'Hey, I saw a vision of her getting shot. By the way, I knew Jeremy was coming home before you did.' Even in my head that sounds mad. They'd admit me to the loony bin and throw away the key. *Forever.*

Panic slowly creeps through my blood. A cold shiver rips up my spine, and I shudder in response to the ice blanketing my body. "I um . . ." Crap, come up with something, Lexi, and fast. " . . . I um . . . She was nice to me when I came out of surgery, and I remember her."

Relief floods both my Mom's and Doris's face. "Oh," Doris breathes. "She was one of the sweetest people," her tone plunges as she looks away from me. When I notice the tears sparkling in her eyes, I feel like kicking myself because I've made her emotional. But I also need to know.

"She was very nice to me."

"Wait, is she the nurse who came out to get me?" Mom looks to me then Doris. I nod my head. "Oh shit," Mom says. "She was shot?" Doris nods, and I'm a second off saying who killed her.

"Have the police said who they think it is?" I push Doris, hoping she'll tell me it's the guy with the scar.

Doris shakes her head. "We aren't privy to such information."

"Did they say anything at all?" Maybe I should tell them what I saw. Damn it, I can't. There's no way they'll believe me. *Ugh, this is so frustrating.* "Is it a guy or girl they're after?" Shit, should I say something?

"They haven't said anything." Doris shakes her head slowly. *Come on, Lexi, tell her.*

My head twists and twirls as a typhoon of thoughts keep plaguing me. I really should do the right thing, but I can't risk people thinking I'm losing my mind either. *Tell them!* My conscience screams at me. *Tell them now.*

I run my hand through my unwashed hair and let out a

pained sigh. "Are you okay?" Mom asks.

The sigh is hiding the turmoil consuming me. "I'm okay." *Tell them,* I scream at myself again.

If I tell them and they don't believe me, then they're going to make me take psychological tests. I'll be prodded and interrogated like I'm a species from another planet. But if I tell them and they do believe me, they'll want to know how I know who the guy is. They'll put me through more tests and I'll be on display like an animal.

I don't know what to do.

Defeated by my own brain, and my own reasoning, I decide not to say anything at all. I can't put myself in a position where I won't be believed.

Relaxing my shoulders, I try and push the feeling of conflict as far down as I possibly can. My parents have always taught me that if I can help someone, I should.

But in this case, if I help Hayley, I'm opening myself up to all types of scrutiny. Pain shoots through my heart, and a sorrow takes me over.

She's dead, because of me.

CHAPTER 5

I'VE BEEN HOME for just over a week, and my body is healing nicely. I haven't returned to school yet, because the doctor told my parents the wound needs to be cared for longer than a normal appendectomy.

I feel good though. And I'm so thankful those stupid vision things I was suffering from have totally disappeared.

Mom and Dad have doted on me. I appreciate it, despite feeling fairly isolated at home. Mom went to the mall, and she refused to let me go with her in case someone knocked into me and opened up my stitches.

But it's okay. I know she's just being protective.

Now I'm getting ready to go back to school. I never thought I'd say this, but, man, I miss school so much.

Dallas Riley is my best friend in the world. She hasn't been able to come and see me, because she's been studying like crazy for exams. Because of that, I've felt even more secluded being stuck at home. We text and call at least a million times a day, but it's not the same.

"You ready?" Mom calls from the kitchen.

I slide my laptop into my school bag and grab my phone from the charger. "Coming," I respond as I look around my room, checking to make sure I haven't left anything behind. I quickly glance at myself in the mirror and smile. I feel like I'm the new girl at school. My nerves rattle with tension and my palms sweat from nervousness. It's an endless cycle.

I'm so happy to be able to get back to school to see Dallas and my other friends.

"Hurry up, Lexi," Mom calls more loudly.

As I approach the kitchen, Mom's head is down while she's rummaging through her bag, flustered at something. I sneak up behind her and lean close into her ear. "No need to shout," I say loudly.

Mom jumps back, clutching her chest. "Jesus, you scared me half to death." She playfully smacks me on the arm. "I think you aged me by about ten years."

"Aging you is okay, as long as you didn't soil yourself in the process."

Mom looks at me and draws her brows together. "You may be a head taller than me, but I can still whoop your butt, young lady."

Leaning down, I plant a kiss on her cheek. Immediately she softens and graces me with a smile. "I know you can," I say, placating her.

"You bet I can. Now hurry up, before we're late." She heads toward the door and waits for me. "You okay?" she asks, concern ringing in every word. "You can stay home for another week, just to make sure everything is completely healed."

"No!" I enthusiastically shout. "I can't stay here anymore. There's really only so much I can watch on Netflix." Rolling my eyes, I dramatize just how boring it is to stay at home. "I'll be fine. Anyway, if it gets to be too much I'll call you, and you or Dad can come pick me up."

Mom's a judge in the local court, and Dad's a bailiff. Their hours aren't always the same, because Mom tends to work late while Dad's home fairly early. But she's arranged to start later in the morning and finish earlier than usual for the next few weeks, because she wants to make sure I'm okay.

"Come on." She checks the expensive watch on her wrist and opens the front door. "But if anything happens, you call me straight away."

"I will, Mom."

"Anything."

"Yes, Mom." I roll my eyes once I'm past her so she can't see.

"Don't roll your eyes at me," she snaps.

Damn it, I hate how she always knows what I'm thinking or doing. "I didn't." *I did.* I smile.

"I know you think I'm being overprotective." *Yep.* "But I'm just worried."

I sink into the passenger seat once Mom unlocks her car with the fob. She's right, she's just being herself. She might be a hard-ass in the court room, but at home she's Mom. I know she loves me and would do anything to protect me.

"I know," I say in a low voice.

Mom pulls out of the driveway and heads toward school. A call comes through on the Bluetooth in the car, and she answers it. It's not unusual for Mom's phone to be continuously ringing, or for her laptop to ding with emails coming through. It's how it's been ever since I can remember: Mom at work and Dad being the primary caregiver. Don't get me wrong, when Mom's needed, she drops everything to make sure Dad and I safe.

She once tried a criminal matter, where the guy being accused was some type of mafia kingpin. That's all she said to me. The only reason she told me was because she hired a body guard for me. Crazy, I know, but she said she had to do it for her peace of mind. That was a few years ago when she was in a more demanding role. She slowed down quite a bit since then.

I stick my headphones on and tune out to the conversation by listening to music. Looking out the window, I watch as the roads lead to school. When we get there, Mom pulls up to the curb. "I'll pick you up," Mom says to me.

"Do you mind if Dallas brings me home?" I ask.

Mom's jaw jumps as she scrunches her mouth together. "As long as you come home after school and don't go anywhere."

"Okay. I'll message you if anything changes, cool?" I ask.

"If you feel any pain . . . or discomfort, or anything at all. Call me, and I'll come to pick you up." *Yes, I know, Mom.*

"Okay."

Mom leans over and gives me a kiss on the cheek.

My face instantly floods with embarrassment. "Oh, my God, Mom. Why did you do that?" I wipe her kiss away and look around to make sure no one saw that.

"Oh, sorry." Mom can never hide her feelings. And right now, I see the hurt splashed deeply across her pretty, older face. And now I feel like a bitch. "If I don't hear from you then I'll assume Dallas will bring you home." She turns forward and slides her sunglasses down.

Damn it. "Thanks for everything, Mom." I lean over and give her a kiss.

Her face lifts with a happy smile. "Thank you," she says. "Have a good first day back at school, sweetheart."

"Bye, Mom." I get out and close the door. Swinging my bag over my shoulder, I head inside to where I know Dallas will be. This time of the morning, she's usually in one of the science rooms, dissecting something or practicing a new formula she's working on.

First thing I do is go to my locker so I can slide my bag in, making sure to take my laptop out for the first classes of the day. With my laptop tucked under my arm, I head over to the science rooms. The corridors are unusually quiet, but it could be because I'm here slightly earlier than normal.

A handful of people walk past me. They're either on their phones, or they look half asleep, like they don't want to be here. As I approach the science lab, I can see the back of Dallas's vibrant purple hair as she's hunched over something. She runs her hand through her hair, and takes a deep breath.

I can't help but smile. She loves purple. Like hardcore loves the stupid color. Even her shoes are purple. Hell, she has purple pens. She has purple hair, a nose ring, several ear rings, and wears purple in everything she owns. Her parents bought her a car for her seventeenth birthday, and it was purple. Her outside doesn't match her insides, though. Her exterior is hard and loud, but she's quiet and super smart. Out of the two of us, she's the one who doesn't need to study, but does.

My parents love her, just like her parents love me. We've been best friends since we were in grade school. She's shy and the sweetest person ever, and I'm known as 'Judge Murphy's daughter,' which means I'm always invited to parties and people are extra nice to me. I can see through their façade, but it doesn't bother me. Dallas and I are super close, and we have a few other friends we hang out with who are cool too.

As soon as I get to the room, I notice the door is open. "For fuck's sake, will you just work?" Dallas grumbles to herself. "Stupid formula, who wrote this anyway? That's right, I did." She slams her hand on the metal counter and huffs in frustration.

"Poor counter," I say as I stand at the door.

Dallas turns her head in a flash, her mouth open with a huge smile curving her lips up. Her eyes widen as she stands with so much force the stool tips over. She runs at me at and slams her body into mine, hugging and squeezing me.

And suddenly, I'm no longer at school. I'm at the mall, walking beside Dallas and a vision copy of me. "He's cute," she says as she stares at the guy walking toward us.

He doesn't look at her though. His eyes are glued to the other version of me. "What's going on?" I ask. I look at my other self, and look at Dallas, desperately trying to get a grasp on reality.

"He's checking you out." Dallas shoulders me.

I watch myself reply, "He's pretty cute."

The guy slows his pace. He's wearing a nicely fitted suit, and is only a little bit older than us, maybe early to mid-twenties. He's clean shaven, with a strong, square jawline, and the most dangerous, dark eyes I've ever seen.

"Oh, my God, you didn't tell me you were coming back today," Dallas says as she pulls out of the hug.

I blink like crazy and try to get my bearings right before I say anything to her. Blankly, I look around and realize I'm out of the damn vision.

"I've gotta go to the bathroom," I say to Dallas and walk as fast as I can to the nearest restroom. When I push the door open, I'm alone. Locking the door behind me, I steady my laptop on top of the hand dryer and go over to the sink to splash water on my face.

I haven't seen anything since I've been home. What the hell is going on? I scoop cold water from the faucet into my cupped hand and splash again. *I don't get it.* Steadying myself against the basin, I stare at my reflection in the graffiti-covered mirror. "No!" No, it can't be real. It was a hallucination from the drugs they'd given me.

There's a pounding at the door and my head snaps to the side. Suddenly I go into panic mode. Crap, this can't be happening. This can't be real. Wake up, Lexi. Wake up from the nightmare you're stuck in. Pinching myself, I don't wake. *This is real.*

Thump. Thump.

I look again at the door and will for myself to wake up.

"Lexi, are you okay? Open the door," Dallas's voice is laced with anguish and fear.

"I'm okay," I call, though the words don't match my stressed tone. I clear my throat and try it again. "I'm okay." It sounds the same, if not worse than my first attempt. Tears begin to well, and my breath flutters erratically.

Calm down, I mentally will myself. I can't open the door like this, she'll know something isn't right and I can't let anyone suspect. I just can't. I don't even know what this is yet, so how can I explain it to anyone else?

I sink against the cool tiled wall and close my eyes. Counting to ten in my head, I take deep breaths.

The continuous hammering on the door is doing nothing to help me settle my frantic nerves. I can't stay in here forever, I have to go out at some stage.

"Lexi, open the door or I'm going to have to call your dad." She's not threatening me, I've known Dallas long enough to know she's saying this because she's worried. "Did you rip your stitches open?"

Pushing off from the wall, my body and mind are finally in a much calmer state. Walking over to the door, I flick the lock. She bursts in and comes straight at me. "I'm okay," I say as I step backward so I can get space between us.

"What happened? Are you okay? Are you in pain?" She steps forward again, her eyes carefully assessing me.

"I'm okay, I just . . ." Shit, what do I say? " . . . you know. I think I just got nervous." Man, I'm clutching at straws.

"You went white and you freaked out. What have you got to be nervous about?" She steps closer and attempts to hug me.

I can't back away from her again. She'll think I'm avoiding her. In this instance, it's a case of it's me not her. But I can't say anything. She probably won't believe me.

Dallas steps closer and pulls me into her arms. The hug is supposed to be innocent and sweet, a touch between best friends. But instead, it's my nightmare.

I'm pulled right back to the mall. Dallas and I are walking together, and Dallas says, "He's cute." I watch Dallas and my vision self and the guy in the expensive, fitted suit walking toward us. "He's checking you out." This time she doesn't shoulder into me but I notice her smirk, and the way she looks between us both.

"So, tell me, how are you feeling?" The breath gets sucked out of me, as I whirl back to the now. *This is killing me.*

"I'm good. I'm ready to get back into things." I walk over to where I had placed my laptop and grab it. The bell rings and we both walk to our first class, math.

"Hey, I need to go to the mall today, I lost my phone charger. Wanna come? I can take you home after."

The hairs on my arms stand to attention while tiny goosebumps rise on my skin. "Yeah, sure. I just gotta let Mom know." Crap. The vision I had may not be real. Maybe I'll sit in the car while she ducks in to get the charger.

Yes, that's exactly what I'll do, because I don't want the vision to come true.

It feels like déjà vu, a sensation of being somewhere before. But in my case. I haven't just got a feeling. I've got clear visions.

Taking my phone out of my pocket, I text to let Mom know Dallas and I are going to the mall and what we're doing.

By the time we reach math, Mom's already responded. *'Be safe and let me know when you arrive home. Dad's working late and will be home by 5pm. I've got a meeting scheduled at 3pm so I'll be later. Order takeout for dinner.'*

Looks like she's working long hours again. *Okay.* I shoot back to her.

The morning goes by quite quickly and as I move through the hallways, I try to avoid touching anyone. But, of course, I can't help it when people aren't watching where they're going.

Damon Scott, one of our school's baseball stars is talking to a few other guys and walks straight into me.

"Watch it, loser," he angrily snaps at me, even though it was his fault.

I'm standing in the hospital; the doctor is talking to a man and a woman I recognize as Damon's parents. "He's torn his meniscus."

"How did he do it?" his mom asks.

"You said he was at baseball practice?"

"Yes," his parents answer in unison.

"And he slid into base right before he said he felt a pop. I'm afraid he's out for the rest of the season. We have to see how bad it is, because he may need surgery."

"Surgery? Will he ever . . ."

I'm back in the corridor, completely stationary as Damon keeps walking past me. "He's going into surgery," I say to myself. I find I speak the words in a low tone, but most importantly, I believe them.

Bringing my hand up to my forehead, I rub at it and let out a deep sigh.

Maybe, just maybe, I'm *not* losing my mind.

CHAPTER 6

"I MIGHT STAY in the car while you go and get your charger," I say to Dallas as we leave the student parking lot.

"I haven't seen you in like forever, so no, you're coming in and I'm treating you to some frozen yogurt."

I turn to look at her. My eyebrows shoot up and I give her a 'what the hell' stare. "Frozen yogurt? Seriously? What are we, twelve?" She laughs at me and shakes her head. "And you saw me all day today. Besides, I don't want frozen yogurt. I'll stay in the car and you can get in and get out."

It's her turn to give me the 'what the hell' look. "I don't think so." She lets go of the steering wheel and points her long skinny finger at me. I tease her by leaning over and snapping my teeth toward her extended digit. "Hey, no biting the driver."

We pull up to a set of traffic lights, and a shiny black car rolls to a stop beside us. The windows are so dark I can't see inside, and the engine is incredibly quiet. It's a new car, something you expect to see in a car chase in a blockbuster movie. I stare at the blackened windows and try to imagine who's navigating such a beautiful piece of machinery. "Hey, try to take off a bit faster than this car, I wanna see who's driving," I say to Dallas, hoping to see in through the windshield.

"Oh, a good ol' fashioned drag race." She revs the engine and grips the wheel.

"Look at that car. There's no way you'll even inch in front of it now. They won't let you. You're revving your car like you're on a racetrack."

"I can so take them." She revs again.

"Don't bother now." She's delusional if she thinks her little purple car, with its purple interior, is going to beat the beautiful, sleek, shiny black car next to me.

I have no idea about cars. They simply don't interest me. But even I know the vehicle beside us would totally destroy Dallas's. *Annihilate* it.

The light turns to green, and the impeccable car smoothly vanishes in front of us—while we're still at the light. "That was anti-climactic." Dallas laughs and continues straight ahead toward the mall.

She chats to me about what I missed at school, what the rumors are about why I wasn't at school and who's done what with who. I tune out thinking about the black car.

"That car was a bit too swank to be around here," I say more to myself than to Dallas.

She stops talking and looks over to me for a second. "What car?"

"The one from the light. Did you think it fit in here?"

"Look around, Lexi, we live in a pretty nice area."

She has a point. We do. Not overly affluent, but definitely better than most areas. But still, something was peculiar about it. It just didn't fit in. It was too nice, too shiny, and just—wrong.

"Yeah, I know," I finally concede. She's right. Maybe this whole hallucination thing is playing havoc with my head. That's gotta be it. It's messing with me.

"Hey, what are we doing for your birthday?"

"Ugh, don't remind me. I really don't want to do anything. Can't we just hang out at home, and do nothing?" I sound like I'm whining, but with everything going on with my unstable head, the last thing I want to be doing is having a party or going out. I need normal to come back to me.

Dallas finds a spot close to the mall and pulls into it. "Come on, we're going shopping."

"You sound so cheesy. I'll wait here, you go ahead." I tilt the passenger seat back, place my feet on the dash and close my eyes, pretending I need to sleep.

"Get your butt out." She tugs on my hand, and I'm back to the vision I had earlier. We're walking in the mall, the cute guy, the 'he's cute.' All of it repeats as clearly and perfectly as it did the first time. "Come on, let's go." She slams the car door, and it jolts me back to the present.

Dallas jogs around to my side, opens the door and goes to grab for my hand. But I quickly snatch it away. "I got it," I grumble to her, but on the inside, I'm freaking out. Because I know there'll be a lot of people, which means people are going to brush past me. Which means a living hell of visions.

"Then hurry up." She takes a step back, watching me as I get out.

"You watching me is freaky. I'm not made of glass," I snap.

She takes another step back. "Who made you so bitchy?"

She's right, I'm taking out my frustrations about my screwed-up mind on her. "Sorry," I mumble.

She makes a beeline straight for Target, while my eyes dart like crazy around me, ready to side-step people to avoid making contact with anyone.

Dallas takes a sharp breath in, and I look over to her to notice the flushed color on her cheeks. "He's cute."

The hair on the back of my neck rises, and a lump of anticipation gathers at the base of my throat.

Oh shit. This is real.

"He's checking you out."

I look in the direction her eyes are firmly staring, and see *him*. The guy with the expensive suit and gorgeous square jawline. It's also right now that I say, 'he's pretty cute.' "He's pretty cute," I involuntarily say when I notice how darkly mysterious his eyes are.

He slows his pace, his eyes glued to me.

Double shit—this is *really* real.

"You'll thank me one day."

"Huh?" Just as I turn to question her, she walks close to me, and trips me in front of the guy.

His hands dart out to catch me.

I'm standing on an isolated dock. There's no moon in the sky, and the darkness is eerie. I hear the sound of a ship cruising through the water. I look around and notice I'm standing near the bridge. The ship is a cargo ship, but not one of those huge ones. More like a transporter.

Looking to my left, I see nothing except a few storage containers stacked on top of each other. Looking to my right, the man with the piercing eyes is walking toward me. He's wearing the same expensive suit. He's on his phone, talking to someone. I can't hear what he's saying, but I can see he's getting closer to me.

He stops about five feet away. "I'm here," he angrily spits into the phone. "I'm giving you two minutes." By the tone of his voice I know it's a deadly threat.

I hear a crack from my left. Turning I see three men come out of the shadows. Their menacing stance tells me this isn't going to be good. The huge guns they're holding confirm how bad this actually is. More men surround the suited guy; this is his death. An execution, he's being erased.

"Run," I yell at the man with the darkened eyes. But he can't hear me. "Ru-"

"Are you okay?" The breath gets knocked out of me as he places me on my feet. I stare into his eyes, shocked at what I saw. He's going to die. There'd be no way he'd escape so much fire power. My heart is frantically beating against my chest, my nerves jumping from what I saw. "Are you okay?" he asks again. Automatically I step back, wanting to avoid him. "I'm sorry, did I do something to you?"

I'm lost for words. Completely unable to speak. What I saw scares me. My hands tremble and my blood turns icy cold.

Silently, I turn and sprint away.

Dallas is steps behind me. "Hey, what happened? You turned white, like you saw a ghost." I can hear her footsteps behind me as she tries to catch me.

Her words rock me to my very core.

Stopping in the middle of the mall, I turn to look at her and I see the guy walking away further in the distance. I can't let another person die. I had the power to help Hayley, and she died because I wasn't brave enough to speak up and save her.

I close my eyes for a few seconds, and fight with my brain. Willing myself, I do what I vowed to never do. I need to go and tell him.

"Wait here a second." I run to catch him before he disappears. As I close in on him, I have no idea what I'm going to say, or even how I'm going to say it. Telling him I saw a vision is beyond mad. If a perfect stranger told me they saw an event which hasn't happened yet, I'd smile sweetly and walk away as fast as I could. But, I have to try.

I see him head to the door and I grab his shoulder. He turns, his eyes landing on me. "Hey," he gruffly says before softening to me.

"I'm sorry about that." I point in the direction of where I fell into his arms.

"Don't worry about it."

Closing my eyes, I take a deep breath and open them to find him staring at me. "I know what I'm about to say is going to sound crazy."

His lips pull up into a smirk. "I've heard a lot of crazy in my life, so it better be good." He teasingly winks at me.

Instantly, the worry leaves me, and by him being so approachable, I'm nearly at ease around him. My shoulders drop and I take another more relaxed breath. "I know you don't know me, and this is going to sound really strange . . ."

"Let's fix that, I'm Jude." He holds his hand out to me. Looking down at it, I know what's going to happen, and I don't want to see him get shot.

"I'm Lexi," I reply without taking his hand.

"Now we know each other, Lexi. What did you want to tell me?" He drops his.

"Tonight, you're going to the docks because you're meeting someone."

His back straightens and his shoulders come up high. He holds his hand up to someone, and I look around to see a tall guy, dressed in a smart suit, with short blond hair step forward. I didn't notice him before, where was he lurking? "How do you know this? Who sent you?"

"No one," I answer defensively. "I warned you this was going to sound crazy. But please, don't go tonight. It's an ambush. There will be men there with guns."

He holds his hand up again. I back away from him, suddenly terrified by him and the huge guy who's now only feet away. "Who told you and what do you know about it?" He steps closer and this simple act petrifies me.

"Nobody said anything, I promise you," fear fuels my voice. "Just, please don't go." I step away further. He holds his hand up to the muscle guy and shakes his head at him. "Please." I turn and I run. I run as fast as my feet will take me, and I avoid everyone in my path.

When I get to Dallas, I turn to look over my shoulder toward where I left the guy, but he's not there. He must have left. He probably thinks I'm a girl who's lost her mind.

"What happened to you? Did you get his number?" Dallas asks and waggles her eyebrows at me.

"No, it didn't work out." Turning, I make my way toward the store we were heading to. "Come on."

"What do you mean 'it didn't work out'? You haven't even gone on a date with him."

"And I'm not going to. It's just not right, you know?"

"Lexi, something's happened to you." My spine stiffens in anticipation of what she's going to say. "You're way more jittery around people. What's going on? Has something happened?"

What can I say to her? This is a secret best kept to myself. "Nothing. I think I'm just tired." I place my hand to my stomach where my small scar is to emphasize my statement.

"Do you want to sit?"

"Nah, let's get your charger and go home."

"Okay," Dallas replies as we head into Target.

As we're passing one of the aisles, I get an idea that could possibly help me. "I want to have a look at something," I say as I head toward the women's clothing section. Dallas follows me, and I stop in front of a rack where they have gloves neatly stacked. "I wonder," I mumble to myself. Sliding a glove on, I turn to look at Dallas who's busy scrolling through her phone.

"Oh, my God!" she nearly shouts, and suddenly becomes much more invested in her phone.

"What?" I step forward hoping to get a glimpse of what's garnered her attention.

"Damon Scott's been stretchered off the field. Apparently, he hurt himself sliding into base in practice."

"And he's torn his meniscus."

"What? All it says on his page is that he's in the hospital. How do you know, Lexi?" Her eyes question me as she looks up from her phone.

Crap, did I say the words aloud? "What?"

"You said he'd torn his meniscus."

"What? Did I? I was just thinking I hope it's not as serious as a torn meniscus because that would mean he'd be out for the rest of the season."

She draws her brows together and slightly tilts her head to the side. Panic rises through me as I wait for the onslaught on questions. "Are you okay?"

Whoa, what a question. I really wasn't expecting it. I honestly thought she was going to hammer me but instead, she genuinely seems concerned. I know Dallas is my best friend, and she'll always have my back, but this secret I have can never get out. It's not something I think anyone can handle. "I'm perfect." I give her a smile, and beg her with my eyes to please drop it. "I promise." I cross my heart.

"As long as you're okay."

"I am." The intensity in her eyes softens and her gaze flicks back down to her phone. A small shallow breath leaves my chest as I prepare to touch her hand. I'm wearing gloves, and I'm hoping I don't get a vision. I'm almost certain this will work, but a slow trepidation quivers inside me.

Reaching out, I hesitantly touch her hand. "What's up?" she asks, looking away from her phone for a brief few seconds.

Relief floods every part of me. "What do you think of these?" I ask, covering up the real reason I touched her hand.

"They're gloves." Her eyebrows come together and she look at me sharply. "They're gloves," she says again, completely bored.

"Yeah, I think I'll buy them."

"Well, buy them. Can I go get a charger now?"

She doesn't realize how thankful I am that this has worked. So now, all I need to do is keep my hands and arms covered and that way I won't have any more visions.

The only problem is, school is almost finished, and this means, summer is really close.

Which means, no long sleeve sweaters or gloves.

Great.

CHAPTER 7

"OH, MY GOD, did you hear?" Dallas asks when I meet her at school the next day.

"Hear what?"

"Damon tore his meniscus sliding into base. Apparently, it was a freak kinda accident. He's not able to finish the season out. He has to have an operation on his knee."

"Yeah, I was with you yesterday when you read it on his wall." I lean against one of the lockers beside hers.

"Yeah, but he put on Facebook this morning it's a definite tear. He's angry he's going to miss out on the rest of the season."

I'd be angry too. "There's always next year." I lift my shoulders in resignation. There's not much they can do, I suppose.

"Man, how crappy would that be? To get nearly to the end of the season, and he goes out on an injury." I lift my shoulders again and clutch my books to my chest. "You must really like those gloves you bought yesterday." She pointedly looks down to my covered hands. "Are you getting sick?" She eyes what I'm wearing today. A thin long sleeved sweater, jeans, and gloves.

"Nah, I'm okay. Just thought the weather looked cooler when I was getting ready for school." It's not true. I know today is inching toward mid-eighties, but if I can get through the last few weeks of school without touching anyone, or too many people, then that means I'll have the entire summer where I can hide away at home and not get any visions.

My phone vibrates in my pocket, and I take it out to see it's Mom calling me. "Hang on," I say to Dallas before answering Mom's call. "Hey."

"Lexi, are you okay?" she asks. Although she's trying to conceal it, I can tell there's panic in her voice.

"Why wouldn't I be?" Ice rips through my spine, and I know Mom doesn't call to ask if I'm okay. Something's off. I can feel it.

"I've called the school and told them you need to come home."

"What? I only just got here."

"Your father is coming for you now, you have to go and wait for him."

My heart is thumping in my chest and the hairs on my arms stand to attention. It's like every one of my senses are on high alert. Someone down the hall drops something heavy on the stark concrete floor. Instantly my head turns to see what's going on, and I know I'm hyper-aware of everyone and everything happening right now. "Mom, you're scaring me." My palms coat in a fine sheen of sweat.

"What's wrong?" Dallas asks. Her brows are drawn together, she's worried.

"The school knows you're going, so get your bag and go wait for your father. No matter who else comes, only get in the car with Dad."

"I have to go, I'll call you later," I say to Dallas as I turn and head toward my locker not waiting to hear Dallas's response. "Okay, I'm going to my locker to get my bag. Mom, please tell me you're alright."

"We're fine, but I need to get you home. I can't leave yet, but I'll be home within the next hour and I'll explain it all then."

"Are you safe?" I ask, really hoping the answer isn't going to freak me out more than I already am.

"For now, I am."

Bile quickly rises to the back of my throat, and now my body has gone into full on panic mode. "For now?"

"I'll stay on the line until Dad gets there. But you have to hurry up."

"Mom, this is really scaring me." I get to my locker, grab my bag, and walk outside. "He's not here yet," I say as I get to the front of the school and look up and down the street for Dad.

"He shouldn't be too long."

"Okay." My breathing changes and in this moment, I feel like I'm lost. Isolated from my family, and hoping everything is okay. I keep looking, and see our car approach from down the street. "He's here." I run down the steps and wait for Dad to pull up at the curb. "Bye, Mom, I'll see you when you get home."

"It's your father?" Her voice is now dripping with concern.

Jesus, what is going on? I see Dad through the front windscreen and wave to him. "Yeah, it's Dad."

"Okay, I'll see you when I get home."

I hang up from Mom and step closer to the curb. Dad pulls up in front of me, and waits 'til I'm inside. He flicks the switch on the driver's door, locking the car. "Dad," I say. I'm desperate to find out what's happening.

He puffs his chest out while releasing a slow, strained breath. "Your mother will be home soon and we'll explain everything."

Ugh, I hate not knowing. "Dad, this whole secrecy thing is scaring me. Put my mind at ease and tell me you and Mom are both okay."

"We're both okay." The crack in his voice sings a different story, and the tension in his shoulders confirms it. He looks over at my hands, and notices the gloves. "You cold?" he asks, concerned.

"I . . . um, wanted to wear them. You know?"

Dad nods his head and presses his mouth into a thin line.

As we drive in silence toward home, Dad keeps looking in the rearview mirror, constantly on high alert. Taking my glove off, I grip his hand hoping to see something, but I get nothing from him. I haven't been able to get anything from either of my parents.

Dad gets home quite quickly and pulls into the driveway, presses the remote for the garage, and rolls his car into it. I get out and head inside just as the garage door is lowering. When I get into the family room, I toss my bag on one of the chairs and sink into our oversized, cream colored sofa. I'm so damn nervous about what's happening, that I try to ease myself by tapping my hand on my leg.

What if they've learnt about these crazy visions I've been having? What if they're going to question me about them? Oh crap, what if they want to send me to a psychiatrist because they think there's something wrong with me?

Is there something wrong with me?

Am I imagining everything I've seen? Am I losing my mind?

The tension inside my body is sending me over the edge with angst and worry. Standing I head down the hall toward my bathroom. "Where are you going?" Dad calls sharply as he appears at the mouth of the hall.

"To the bathroom." Yeah, like his tone isn't scaring the crap out of me, or the fact he's even asked. Now I know, for sure, something is going on.

"Don't go outside the house."

My palpitating heart increases in its constant thumping against my chest cavity. "I won't." *What is going on?*

I lock myself in my bathroom, and go over to the vanity. I let the faucet run, ensuring the water is as icy cold as it can be before splashing it onto my face. Taking a deep breath, I look up to the mirror and stare at my reflection.

My dark brown hair is pulled back into a high ponytail, and my normally clear complexion is splotched with redness. My green eyes are marked with visible red veins. Anyone looking at me can see the tension, the stress, and the worry.

I stay in here for a while, examining my face. All I know is my pulse is rapidly vibrating through my body and my heart won't calm. *What if they know?*

As I'm splashing water on my face, there's a sharp rapping at the door. It makes me jump in fright, while my blood chills in anticipation.

"Lexi," Mom's normally smooth voice sounds panicked. "I'm home."

I don't even bother drying my face, instead I throw the door open and launch myself into her arms. She easily accepts my body being flung into her petite frame. "What's going on? I'm so scared," I whisper.

"Everything will be okay, but there are some changes coming for the next few months."

She leads me out to the family room, where Dad's sitting and by the front door is a heavy-set guy in a suit that doesn't fit him properly. His arms are crossed in front of his chest, and he eyes me suspiciously as we walk out to join Dad.

"What's going on?"

Please don't tell me you know. Please.

Dad pats the huge sofa cushion beside him, and I move to sit. Mom grabs one of the chairs from the dining room and brings it over to sit between Dad and me. "Okay." She takes a deep breath, looks to Dad then starts, "I've been working on a case that is sensitive."

My brows furrow together and suddenly I'm relieved this has nothing to do with me, and what I've been experiencing. "Okay." I drag the word out, still skeptical although somewhat comforted. Both emotions drag through me, I'm happy it's not me, but worried as well.

"The case has become quite volatile."

"Volatile? How?" I look to Dad and he gives me a weak smile.

"I can't discuss it, however, there will be a few changes happening."

"Like what?"

"Like, Marcus." Dad points to the guy by the door, who's been standing still as a statue.

"What about Marcus?"

"He's going to be your bodyguard."

"My what?" I nearly yell. "I don't need a bodyguard."

"Unfortunately, Lexi, yes you do. You really do," Dad's voice softens and I can hear the fear radiating from him.

"What does this mean?" I look back over to Marcus. "For how long?"

"Until the case is finished, and then maybe some time after that too," Mom answers.

"And I suppose you can't tell me why I need him?" I point to Marcus; whose immobile expression tells me he's heard my questions many times before.

"I can't say anything right now, although you'll probably hear all about it over the next couple of weeks."

"Mom," I let out a long-drawn breath. "Are you going to be okay? Are you and Dad safe?"

"We'll be fine, because we have security assigned to us, too," Dad says.

Instantly my head whips around to look at Marcus again. "Where are they?" Marcus remains stoic. He says nothing. *He's a chatty guy.*

"They're outside. Marcus will be your bodyguard and will accompany you everywhere you go. I don't want you going anywhere without him."

"Madam, if I may?" *He speaks,* Marcus actually speaks.

He's an older guy, around the same age as my parents. The lines around his eyes tell a tale of the things he's seen. And I figure they're things no human would want to see. There's something about him, a small, niggling feeling eating away at me.

"Of course, please," Mom answers Marcus's question.

He steps forward, and starts to speak in his deep, gruff voice. "Miss Murphy, I've done this many times, and I can guarantee you, I won't be a nuisance to you at school. And I certainly won't cause you any embarrassment."

Standing I head over to him. I need to know for sure that he can be trusted. "It's rude of me not to introduce myself." I stick my hand out to him, and wait for him to accept it and for the vision to happen.

He extends his hand, wraps his fingers around mine.

And I'm in his vision. He's alone in a car, there's no noise, no music, no voices. He's got a dark pair of glasses over his eyes and he sits rigidly, driving.

I look around to see where we are, but it's dark and there's no light anywhere. This is so bizarre. There are no landmarks, no hints as to where he is. Desperately I search for something, *anything*. But I'm not getting any clues.

I'm back in my family room, and Marcus looks at me with suspicious eyes. His gaze slowly goes down to my hands, as the corner of his mouth draws up in the smallest and creepiest tug. "I think we're going to get on just fine, Judge Murphy."

Terror enshrouds me. He's hiding something and I'm not sure what. How could he be driving and there was no noise, no sound, nothing in the background? How is that even possible? And why is he wearing dark glasses to drive at night? He's definitely hiding something.

"Yeah, Mom, I'm sure Marcus and I will be fine." I'm not going to say anything to my parents. First, they'll think something's wrong with me, second, they wouldn't understand and third, there's a rock sitting in the pit of my stomach that tells me, this is about me. All about me.

And all about my gift.

A gift I now accept as part of me, and a gift I know no one can ever find out about.

CHAPTER 8

"**A**RE YOU READY, Miss Murphy?" Marcus asks as he stands by the front door.

My parents have left to go to work already, and are entrusting Marcus with my safety. I'm okay with this, because it means my parents are away from here and away from him.

Mom told me last night, Marcus is my main bodyguard, and there's another person, a woman by the name of Laura who'll be on guard through the evening until Marcus returns in the morning.

I didn't meet Laura last night, apparently, she stays outside my bedroom window. *Weird, I know.*

"Grabbing my bag." I slip my gloves on, and slide a thin long-sleeved sweater over my shoulders.

He waits by the front door, and when I approach him, he opens it for me. "It's a beautiful day outside." He looks me over, his glance taking in my gloves and long-sleeved sweater.

"It is," I reply with a saccharine smile.

As I walk through the door, I feel his hand go to my lower back. Instantly, the hair on the base of my neck stands to attention. I whip my head around and glare at his offending hand. He snatches it away, but his eyes are looking straight at me.

Something is so off about him. I don't know what it is yet, but

I'm going to find out.

We get to the car, and he opens the front door for me. I opt to get in the back, and away from him. I don't like him. I've still got this niggling feeling in the pit of my stomach.

"I hear it's your birthday soon," he says as we start toward school.

"It is."

"Are you and Dallas doing anything special for it?"

Icy cold shards rip up my spine when he mentions Dallas's name. "Not sure." It's like he's trying to tell me he knows a lot about me, maybe even warning me.

"If you and Dallas do something, then I'll have to accompany you." Yep, a definite warning.

A smile jerks on my lips, I feel like being a smart ass to him. "Anywhere we go?"

"My orders are to ensure your safety." He stops talking, but I can sense he wants to say more.

"Dallas and I might hang out in the girls' bathroom."

"Then I'll wait for you outside the door."

"You're not squeamish, are you? We're girls; we talk about all kinds of things."

He chuckles and shakes his head. "There's nothing you can say to make me squirm. I've heard it all. I've been trained . . ." He pulls away from the sentence before he continues.

Interesting. "You've been trained to . . . ?" I question.

"I've been trained to be discreet," his voice changes into a flatter, more reserved tone.

"Okay," I reply, knowing that's not what he wanted to say.

We arrive at school and Marcus parks toward the front. I'm out and walking away without waiting for him. I'm sure he has my class schedule and he knows where I'm going. He seems to know a lot about me, without me telling him.

I head into the science room to find Dallas; whose purple hair looks more vibrant today then yesterday.

"Girl," she yelps the moment she sees me. "What the hell happened? I tried calling you but your phone was switched off." I hear the footsteps and know, Marcus is standing behind me. Dallas's brown eyes look at him, then me, then back to him. "Can I help you?" she asks as she steps forward and in front on me.

"He's with me," I say before Marcus can respond.

She turns and looks at me. Now we've swapped positions, and I'm looking at Marcus while Dallas's back is to him. "What's going on? What's with the heavy?" She thumbs over her shoulder.

"A few things are going on with Mom and her work, so he's here for me."

She crinkles her nose and leans in to whisper, "He goes everywhere you do?"

"Afraid so." I nod my head and smirk at her.

"Everywhere?"

Marcus remains impassive and cold with his features. "Yep, everywhere."

"Ugh." She sighs and slumps her shoulders. "Well that sucks, having a babysitter, but, anyway." She shrugs and smiles at me. "I may as well introduce myself." Her eyes widen and she plasters a fake smile on her face. Turning quickly on her heels, she walks over to Marcus and sticks her hand out waiting for him to take it.

Marcus looks down at her hand, as if it's contaminated. "He's not very vocal or accommodating," I announce from behind her.

"Hi, I'm Dallas, and I'm Lexi's best friend." He continues to stare at her, cool and unresponsive. "I'm not going away until you shake my hand and introduce yourself." She juts her hand out further to him. He continues to stare at her, blinking occasionally.

Walking toward her, I can see her smile growing even further. She's so infectious and has the biggest heart known to man.

"He's a robot," I say to Dallas.

Marcus's brows draw together in the slightest of movements. His mouth only just pulls at the corners. "Marcus," he announces in his deep 'don't mess with me' voice. But he refuses to shake her hand.

Which intrigues me even more, because I know with me, he was the complete opposite.

"See, it wasn't that bad, was it?" Dallas teases, but her hand drops beside her, unsuccessful at garnering any more than a one word answer.

Marcus goes back to looking like a statue.

The bell sounds. Dallas grabs her bag and we head to our first class, which happens to be English.

As we get into class, Marcus also enters and stands at the back of the room. My face flames, and my eyes widen while I look around at the class and notice everyone's staring at him.

I stand and walk over to him, completely embarrassed. "You have to stay outside the door."

"No." He straightens his back and looks ahead, past me.

"Marcus, you're going to embarrass me. Please, stand outside the door," I say, more firmly.

He continues to look past me. With his deadpan face, and deep, gruffly voice, he adds, "No."

"Ugh," I grumble as I take my phone out of my pocket and head out into the hallway. My shadow is only feet away from me.

Dialing Mom's number, she picks up virtually straight away. "Is everything okay?" there's panic creeping into her voice.

"Mom, Marcus is standing in my classroom. In it! Not outside the door, he's inside. Ugh, can you tell him to go out in the hallway? It's embarrassing."

"Sorry, sweetheart, but your safety is my only concern. I really don't care if it's cool or not, the fact is, with him there, you're safe."

Looking over to Marcus, who's still standing like a statue, he grins—as if he knows what Mom's said. "Mom," I plead with her.

"Sorry, but no," her voice becomes hard. She's using her 'judge' voice on me. I hate it when she does that, because it scares the crap out of me.

Yes, I know. I'm nearly seventeen and scared of my mommy. I've heard how some hardened criminals are petrified of her, so what chance do I stand when she goes all authoritarian on me?

"Mom," I try my hardest again.

"Is that all, Alexa?"

Damn it, she's using my full name. Now I know there's no more discussing this matter. "Yes, Mom," I mumble, defeated.

"If you need anything, call me, okay?"

Yeah right, I do need something, for G.I Joe to stand outside the classroom and not inside where everyone is going to question me about who he is and what he's doing here. "Yes, *Mom*."

She hangs up without saying anything else, and I huff in frustration. I walk past a smug Marcus. "Am I to stay outside?" he asks in a challenging tone.

Jerk.

"You already know the answer."

I head back into the classroom, where Miss Edwards has already started the class. "Nice of you to take time out from your important phone call to join us. Next time I'll write you up. Sit." She points to my seat with a scowl on her face.

I hear Marcus chuckle from behind me, and I swing around to give him an 'eat me' look. Instead, the jerk winks at me, smiles and stares ahead.

Double *ugh*. Dealing with him is going to be painful.

Quietly I sit, and face forward. My jaw is clenching and I'm shaking because I'm so mad with Mr. Steroid and his smug attitude.

"As I was saying before I was rudely interrupted, today's an extra fun day because I'm giving you all an exam on the book we've been studying." The entire class, including me, groan. "If you've read *To Kill a Mockingbird* then you'll do well, if you didn't, then you won't." The class mumbles again. I know I've read it, well kind of skim-read it.

She starts handing out the tests, and gets to my desk. She places the test face down on my table, and simultaneously I reach for my pen. Our hands touch in error, and suddenly I'm sitting in this quaint airy office space.

Looking around I see a library from floor to ceiling. Every spare space has been taken up with books. The office is light and bright, painted a happy tone of yellow. The furniture is white and a stark contrast to the heavy wooden cases containing easily hundreds if not a thousand books.

Directly in front of me is Miss Edwards, at her desk. She's rubbing at her temples with her left hand, as she writes something with her right. I stretch over and look at what she's writing. On top of the page she's written, 'Points that need mentioning,' I look down the list and realize she's written down what we need to mention in order to receive high marks. I quickly read as many as I can before I'm forced out of this vision. I recite them as I go along, trying to commit each and every one to memory.

I'm back in the classroom and Miss Edwards moves to the next student.

I didn't get to see them all, but I think I saw enough to remember how she wants us to answer the questions. Slyly I turn to look around the class preparing for the test. Marcus catches my eye, and he lifts his brows and gives me a small nod.

Crap.

Crap.

Double crap.

He knows.

CHAPTER 9

Marcus, AKA my shadow, AKA G.I. Joe, AKA anything I feel like calling him, has not left my trail at all. Even going to the bathroom, he's positioned himself outside the door and called out when I've taken too long.

When I get home from school, I want to touch him and try to get another read on him. Try to get to know him. But something tells me, this is going to be harder than I can imagine.

Sitting in the cafeteria at lunch, I'm pushing my food around the plate while Dallas, Courtney and Amy talk about what happened last weekend. I can hear them, but I'm definitely not listening.

"Lexi." I feel a tap on my shoulder.

Turning I'm met by Brody Williams who's one of the guys in my year. He looks nervous, like he's about to puke on me. "Hey, Brody," I say as I offer him a smile.

"How are you?" He rubs his hands down the front of his jeans, and looks to the floor.

"Yeah, good." I notice Marcus step forward, moving beside Brody.

Brody looks to Marcus and his face drains, as he swallows hard. "Um, I just wanted to see how you are." He looks to me, then back to Marcus, then over to his friends who are sitting a few tables away.

Brody Williams is one of the really smart kids at school, like super smart. He wears the cutest glasses, and has the absolute most horrific fashion sense ever. He wears plaid and stripes together. But he's really cute, and super nerdy.

"I'm doing well. Want to sit?" I point to the empty chair beside me.

"Um," he nervously answers as he looks over to Marcus. "Um." Marcus's eyes narrow to Brody, and Brody retaliates by stepping backward.

"Just sit."

Carelessly forgetting, I reach out to grab his hand, and I'm thrust inside a vision. He's sitting at a table while his mom's in the kitchen behind him. "You have three more hours of study to do tonight, Brody," his mom calls from in front of the stove.

"I know, Mom," he replies and sighs. She turns her back to continue cooking, and Brody slumps further down into his chair. I can see the spread of books out on the table, while his laptop is opened and he's working on something. "I'm tired. Can I put in an extra hour tomorrow and take an hour off tonight?"

"Do you want to end up like your father?" his mother spits toward him. He shakes his head. "Do you want to end up with a needle in your arm, like your brother has?"

Brody sighs and shakes his head again.

I can feel the heaviness in the room. The immense amount of pressure on him to do well at school. "I'm just tired and I want a rest."

His mom marches over from the kitchen, and stands with her hands on her hips, towering over him. "If you don't educate yourself, you'll never get anywhere in this life. You understand?" she half yells at him.

"Yes, Mom," he replies in a small and meek voice.

But even I can see, he's miserable and probably burnt out from studying. She lets out a long exhale, pats him on the head, and says, "Okay, take a break for an hour. You can go practice your saxophone."

For a split-second I see the happiness in Brody's eyes, before the fire is extinguished the moment his mom gave him another task. "Sure." He pushes up from the table, and leaves where he was studying. His mom returns to the kitchen, and I hear a beautiful and soulful song being played from another area of the house.

His mom bursts into tears in the kitchen. She stops doing what she was doing, and looks up to the ceiling. "His only hope to get out of here is for him to study hard. Please, Daddy, please help him find his way." Her words are heartfelt, and I can tell she's just doing the best she can.

Looking around the house, I notice it's a in run-down condition. The furniture is all old and worn. But what is really apparent is she's doing the best she can.

I blink and I'm back in the cafeteria. Brody's still standing in front of me, looking the way he was before my vision. "Here, sit," I offer again.

Brody sits and nervously knots his hands together. "Thanks. Um, how are you feeling? I heard you were rushed into the hospital. Are you better now?"

"Yeah, I'm great. So how long have you been playing the saxophone?"

His eyes light up, his chest puffs out and a genuine smile brightens his entire face. "I've been playing for years. Mom said I had to pick an instrument to play, so I picked the sax. How do you know I play the sax?"

Great, I need to lie. "Didn't I see you in band once?"

He shakes his head. "Maybe."

After that, the conversation between Brody and me becomes easier. Marcus steps back and resorts to only staring at Brody as opposed to actively intimidating him. I come to learn Brody likes Dallas, and wants to ask her out on a date but has no idea how to do it. While Dallas was preoccupied with talking to Courtney and Amy, he wanted to ask me what she likes—other than purple.

When he leaves, I feel different. The vision I had from Brody was more defined, and I took more in. I noticed more details and I spent extra time in there even though the touch was only slight.

Feeling happier, I turn to eat some of my food before lunch is finished and we need to head back to class.

"Hey," Dallas says staring at me.

"What?" Her intense glare is scaring the crap out of me. I wipe my nose in case I have something hanging. And then I run the back of my hand over my mouth.

"You wearing contacts?" She moves her face closer to mine, and really stares into my eyes.

"Ahhh, no. I don't need glasses."

"I know you don't need glasses, but have you got colored contacts in?"

"Dallas, I swear you're the weirdest person I know. Why would I have colored contacts when there's nothing wrong with my eyes?"

"Dude, seriously, it looks like that eye has a colored contact." She points to my left eye. "It's kinda got a tinge of blue around the outside."

"What?" Stressing out, I jump up from my seat, leave my tray and head over to the closest female bathrooms. I know Marcus is only paces behind me because I can hear the heaviness of his footsteps on the hallway floors.

Pushing through the bathroom door, there are two girls standing near the basin, re-applying their make-up. They turn to look at me, and one arches her brow as I frantically head toward an unoccupied mirror.

They both go back to talking, something about what one of the cheerleaders did with another cheerleader's boyfriend. I tune out as I closely approach the mirror and check my eyes out.

I've always had freaky colored green eyes, they're an intense green with small, darker green outline. My parents have no idea where I got the coloring from, because both come from generations of brown, or dark brown eyes. Mine have always been so different that I used to get teased in elementary school all the time about them.

Now I get the occasional compliment, and sometimes people ask me if the color comes from contacts.

Leaning into the mirror, I focus on my left eye, and notice the blue around one side of the iris. It's definitely there, and quite prominent considering my eyes are such a weird and vibrant shade of green. The blue is a glaring contrast to the green surrounding it.

"Why are you blue?" I ask aloud.

"What?" one of the girls grunts.

I'd completely forgotten all about them until the one with the long blonde hair, and perfect porcelain skin speaks.

Blinking, I turn to look at her. "I was talking to myself." Spinning back, my gaze goes directly to my right eye. "How weird."

Scrunching my brows together, I try and make sense of my left eye. I'm nearly seventeen, my eyes shouldn't be establishing their color now. This is so freaky, and not to mention, creepy.

Taking a deep breath, I'm completely intrigued by the blue.

The two girls exit the bathroom, leaving me the only person in here. Stepping back half a step, I tilt my head to the left and then to the right. Yep, it totally looks weird, but I kinda really like it too.

The door swings open forcefully, and Marcus steps into the bathroom. "Alexa," he booms as he looks around the bathroom with a drawn weapon.

The power of the door slamming up against the wall, frightens me, making me jump. "Jesus, Marcus, you scared the shit out of me." My heart beats frantically as I clutch at my chest in a mini panic attack.

"Are you alright?"

I squint my eyes at him and slant my head to the side. "Why wouldn't I be? And why have you got your gun out? Why the hell have you got a gun to begin with? We're in a high school, there's no need for weapons. And . . ." I just feel like yelling at him, so I continue, " . . . what if I was on the toilet?"

Marcus straightens, holsters his gun, and buttons his suit jacket up. "I'm doing my job."

"By nearly making me soil myself?" I point toward his chest where his holster is.

He chuckles, runs his hand through his very short hair and shakes his head. "I'll wait for you outside."

"Yeah, good idea, buddy," I angrily spit.

Marcus leaves me in the bathroom, and I take a minute to calm down and get ready to go to class. As I leave Dallas and Marcus are both outside the door, talking. "Hey, you okay?" Dallas asks. "You ran off and I had no idea why."

"I um, you know, I um thought I had something in my eye." I rub it for extra effect. "I'm good." We both head toward our next class, and I look over my shoulder to Marcus. "What were you two talking about?"

"He was telling me about a time a client he was protecting ran him over because she was drunk."

More like, because he's an ass. "He doesn't strike me as a guy who has a conversation easily," I grumble that he's talking to her and only giving me snide or blank stares.

"I don't know." She shrugs nonchalantly. "I asked him if he's ever been a body guard to a girl before, and he told me about the drunk chick."

"Hmm, interesting," I mumble as I look over my shoulder again to Marcus.

We head into class, and Marcus stands at the back of the room.

Something is definitely off about him, and I want to know what it is.

CHAPTER 10

IT'S BEEN DAYS since Dallas first told me about my eye color. I haven't had another vision, because I haven't touched anyone.

Every time I try to touch Marcus, so I can get a better read on him, he always maneuvers away from me so I can't touch him. He's a strange man, a man I'm convinced knows much more about me than he's letting on.

It's my birthday in four days, and I can't wait 'til I turn seventeen. My parents already told me, they're going to buy me a car as soon as I get a permit. I can't wait!

I leave my bedroom and go in search of my parents. "Mom," I call loudly. "Dad!" I call even louder.

"They had to leave early this morning," Laura replies from the kitchen.

She's stealthy, quietly tip-toeing through the house, sneaking around like a damn cat.

I head into the kitchen to find her leaning against the island counter, drinking a cup of coffee. "Where's Mr. Personality?" I ask as I look around.

The corners of her mouth tug up in a small smile, but she quickly lifts the cup to cover her grin. Her eyes though, they're still smiling. "He'll relieve me later today," her reply is short.

"Great," I mumble to myself. Heading into the kitchen to grab some breakfast, I decide I want to peek into Laura's future. "We haven't really been introduced." I hold my hand out to her. "I'm Alexa Murphy but everyone calls me Lexi." Not that she doesn't know this, but it's a way for me to grab hold of her hand.

She looks down at my offered hand and arches her brow at me. "You can call me Laura," she says without taking my hand.

I shove it further forward, and hope she takes it. She stares into my eyes, then places her cup on the counter. She wraps her fingers around my hand, and in that very instant, I'm standing in a dark alley.

Graffiti adorn the walls as a putrid smell wafts into my nostrils.

"Come on, I'm going to buy you dinner," Laura says to someone. I can't see who she's talking to because Laura's standing with her back to me, and it's blocking whomever she's speaking with.

"Just give me the money, and I'll buy my own dinner," a soft voice replies.

"We both know the moment I give you money, it's going in your arm, so no. Come with me to the diner around the corner and I'll buy you something to eat."

The darkness of the alley frightens the shit out of me. The fearsome sounds coming from close by terrify me more than the murky shadows. My frantic heart doesn't get the memo that this is a vision. It's so real.

"I can't go there." The girl steps around Laura and starts to move away from her. Her features are almost identical to Laura's, except Laura has dark hair, and this girl has dull, lifeless brown hair. The girl pulls away from Laura, and rubs her right hand up and down her left arm.

She's so dirty, and her clothes are barely hanging together. "Why?" Laura questions. "Why can't you go there?" I glimpse at Laura, then look back to her, studying her features. She has a split lip with tiny blood droplets still fresh from where it's been cut. Her left eye is heavily bruised, almost swollen shut, while her right eye has darkening splotches beneath it. She looks like she's gotten a few punches from someone.

The girl looks down at her feet and shuffles. She looks like she wants to go to the bathroom, but I know she's nervous about telling Laura the reason. "Because . . ." her small voice trails off.

My heart breaks for the girl. She's obviously a junkie and she's so embarrassed by the way her life has turned out for her.

"It's not too late for you," I say while trying to reach out to her. But of course, she can't hear me.

"Just come home with me, Jade. I can get you the help you need. Please? It's not safe out here." The fear Laura has for her sister's predicament is obvious.

Laura's begging brings tears to my eyes. Jade's shoulders slump and she shakes her head. "This is my home now." She sweeps her hand across the dirty, disgusting alleyway. "This is where I belong."

"No, it doesn't have to be. Come home. I'll get you into a treatment program. I'll help you with everything. Just please come home."

Jade straightens her shoulders and lifts her chin. "If you want to do something for me, then give me some money," her voice turns harsh, but the tear that escapes her eye tells such a different story.

"You know I won't do that."

"Then I have to go to work." She shrugs out of the dirty sweater she's wearing and ties it around her tiny waist. As she walks past me, I notice the track marks and the bruising prominent on her arms.

"Jade."

I'm back in my kitchen. Laura leans over and picks her coffee cup up.

It's then I see the stress on her face, the worry in her eyes, and the wrinkles across her forehead. She looks so tired, like she needs to sleep for a hundred years to catch up. What do I say to her? Nothing, because if I do, she's going to question how I know about Jade. She's going to want to know and I can't give her any answers.

"I won't be long, I'll just grab an apple and some juice and we'll get going to school."

"Sure thing." She finishes her coffee and walks over to the sink, where she fills the cup with water and leaves it in the basin. "I'll wait for you outside."

As I lean against the counter, drinking my juice, I can't help but feel so sorry for Laura. She must have one tough life, but then again, not tougher than Jade's.

Jade's addicted to drugs, that much I know. But what would make a person turn to drugs to begin with? The most frustrating thing about my visions, is that I only get a snippet of them. I haven't been able to pinpoint why I get shown those moments in time.

Pushing away from the counter, I grab my bag and head to the front door. Locking it behind me, I make my way over to the car. Laura is sitting in the driver's seat and the car is idling while she waits for me.

I get in the back and shut the door. "Seat belt," she says sternly.

"Yeah, I know," I bite back a little too angrily. Considering all the crap she's going through in her personal life, I should cut her a bit of slack. "Sorry."

She reverses out of the driveway, and gives me a quick nod of acceptance.

We drive to school in silence, and I spend the minutes looking out at the familiar streets, the same cars, and the recognizable house.

A beautiful black car pulls up beside us at the light, and I instantly identify it as the same one I saw when Dallas and I went to the mall. "Huh," I sigh.

A gorgeous car like that is not easy to forget.

"You okay?" Laura asks from the front seat.

"Yeah, just thinking."

The light turns green, and the sleek black vehicle peels away into the left lane and speeds ahead.

"Care to share?"

My eyes are glued to the way the car hugs the road. "Nah, it's okay." The car disappears, and I'm left still watching the direction it when in.

My head leans back against the headrest, and I close my eyes as we make the final few miles to school.

Suddenly, we're hit hard from behind. We're hit with so much force that my head jolts forward as my seat belt locks firmly into place. I hear glass shattering, and the crumping sound of the body of the car.

"Ahhh," I cry in pain as I attempt to bring my hand up to rub my throbbing neck.

We're hit again, with less force, but the impact still makes the car jar forward. My head whips to the side, smashing into something hard.

"What's happening?" I call as a cloak of darkness quickly closes over me. "Laura?" I desperately shout. I get no reply, and my vision clouds over into total darkness.

There's something dripping on my face, but my heavy arms can't wipe at it.

There's noise.

White noise.

People yelling. People talking.

"Be careful!" someone shouts. My weighted body is being moved.

I try to force my eyes to open, but the darkness isn't letting me go. It has its hooks in me, and it's not giving any part of me back.

"Be careful!" the same person yells again.

Flittering my eyelids open, then quickly closing them again, I'm laying down in the back of a car. A car with tall sides and a high roof. *A van.*

But it doesn't look like the inside of an ambulance. It doesn't have all the medical equipment and ambulance carries.

Trying to turn my head, I feel the ache and throbbing increase. "Ahh," I cry in pain.

"There's a doctor waiting for you. Don't move," says a faceless man.

My eyes flicker, then shut as I lose consciousness.

I just hope this is a dream and not a nightmare.

Opening my eyes, I look around. I'm in a light-yellow room, and the sun is beaming in through the large window. The room is light and breezy, almost like I'm in a resort.

Wasn't I in the back of an ambulance? This doesn't look like a hospital room to me.

I move to my side, where I see an opened door leading into a master bathroom. Perplexed, I slowly sit up in bed. "Crap," I say as I rub at a sensitive part of my shoulder. Trying to turn my head, I feel the stiffness and an acute pain shoots up the column of my neck. Standing, I turn to see another two doors. One beside the bathroom, and one on the adjacent wall.

Heading to the one beside the bathroom, I open it to find a huge walk-in closet lined from top to bottom in jeans, t-shirts, shorts, shoes, everything. "What's going on?" I ask myself. "Where am I?"

I don't touch any of the clothes, because I'm not sure who it all belongs to, or even whose room I'm in. Considering the two doors in the bedroom lead to a bathroom and a walk-in closet, I can only assume the third is the way to get out.

My body is stiff and sore, so moving at a rapid pace is not possible. I get to the third door, place my hand on the handle and get . . . nothing.

It's stuck and not moving. "Hello!" I yell and bash on the door. I'm met with silence. "Hello!" I scream even louder.

Panic rises through me as I realize I'm locked in this room and

I can't get out.

Pounding on the door, tears sting my eyes and tumble over as sheer terror ices my veins. "Hello!"

My relentless beating on the door only makes me tire quickly. Moving away from the door, I sit on the large bed and stare at the door with tears streaming down my cheeks.

A huge lump forms in my throat as the tears keep falling. My hands vigorously shake as questions keep coming at me. Why am I here? Why can't I get out? Do my parents know? What's happening?

The door unlocks from the outside; I spring to my feet and move as far away as I can get from the door. Looking around the room, I try to find somewhere to hide. I lift the edge of the blanket, and notice there's no space under the bed. I try the bathroom, but there's no lock on the door. I try the closet; there's no lock on that door either.

I have nowhere to go. Nowhere to hide.

The door slowly opens, and I notice a bedside lamp. I try to snatch it off the top of the small chest of drawers, but it's glued down. "Are you kidding me?" I shout.

I arm myself with the only thing I can, my shoe.

"I'm armed!" I yell at whoever is about to walk in.

I have a death grip on my shoe, no one is going to touch me.

"I'm not going to hurt you," says a male's voice in a calm tone.

"I'm going to hurt you!" I yell at him. He comes into the room and closes the door. "You?" I say, but don't ease up on my pose. My hand is high, ready to smack him with my shoe.

"I apologize for the way you've come to me."

It's the guy from the mall. The one I saw getting ambushed down at the dock. "You're not dead," I say, swallowing back the spit gathering in my mouth. My heart is palpitating and my hands are shaking, but I will do what I need to get the hell away from here.

He holds his hands up to me, trying to show me he's not a

threat. But a threat is exactly what he is. Why would he bring me here? "No, I'm not dead, thanks to you." He slowly moves over toward the window, and sits on the bench beneath it. He sits, and still has his hands up in defense. "I promise, I won't hurt you." I look to the door, and inch toward it. "You won't make it a foot outside that door." He points to where I'm looking. "There's a security guard there." I frown at him and I'm taken aback by his words. "Please, see for yourself."

With my raised shoe, I tiptoe over to the door. When I open it I'm faced with this guy who's huge, and scary. He draws his gun on me, his eyes glued to mine.

My body shakes in response to having a gun pointed at me.

"Put it away," the guy from the mall booms at the guy with his gun drawn.

He immediately holsters it, and goes back to just looking scary not actually threatening me.

"What's going on?" My hands shake so much it looks like I'm trying to swat someone with my shoe.

"Please, put your weapon down," the mall guy says with humor in his voice. "I won't hurt you, and neither will anyone else."

Backing away from the door, I slowly lower my hand, but smash my body up against the wall opposite mall guy. "What's going on? How are you still alive?"

He scrubs his hand over the stubble on his chin and smiles at me. "Please, sit. Are you hungry? Thirsty?"

I stay rooted to the same spot. "You don't own me," I spit toward him.

He chuckles and shakes his head. "Well, about that."

"You don't own me!" I yell at him. "Who the hell do you think you are?"

"Look . . ." He takes a deep breath. "Please, just sit so I can explain what's happening here." He motions between us.

"I'll stay where I am." I raise the shoe again. He chuckles and quickly catches it before it turns into a laugh. But I don't see anything funny about this situation. "What the hell is going on?"

"My name is Jude Caley."

I look away from him for a second. *Jude Caley?* I know that name. I try to search my memory of where I've heard his name before. "Where do I know you from? Other than the mall?"

"I may have a small reputation."

I look to the door where the guy with the gun is. "You think?" I sarcastically say. "I'd say if you have to hire people with guns, you'd probably have more than a 'small reputation.'"

"I really like your sass," he says and laughs again.

His laughing does nothing to soothe me. As a matter of fact, it scares me even more. A man who surrounds himself with people with guns, and says he has a small reputation is most likely the devil or the devil's apprentice.

"I don't give a damn what you like about me. Just tell me what I'm doing here and what you want with me."

"You're an important person to me, Lexi."

"How do you know my name?"

"I know a lot about you. But, you did tell me your name when we met at the mall."

"Just tell me what you want with me." I throw my shoe at him in frustration. He ducks and it hits against the window, which doesn't shatter. *Ugh.*

He stands, picks my shoe up and holds it out to me. "I'm not going to hurt you." He prods the shoe closer to me, but doesn't move. He's waiting for me to crawl closer to him and take it.

"Throw it." I point to the floor. I have no doubt if he wanted to cause me pain, the bed between us wouldn't even be an obstacle for him. He'd get to me in a few leaps, and hurt me. But he hasn't done anything threatening, other than actually keeping me locked in here.

He throws my shoe gently, and it lands with a small thud on the floor. No use in me using it as a weapon. I slide it on, but don't move away from the wall. "What's happening?"

"The day at the mall, you told me not to go to the docks because it was an ambush. There's only one way you could've known about it, and that was if you were aware of who I am, and my business dealings."

"I still have no idea about your business dealings. Though judging by the fact there's a guy standing outside my door with a gun, I'm guessing your business doesn't exactly file a tax return."

He smirks and he gives me a small nod. "Let's just say, you're not too far from the truth."

"Hmm, figures."

"As I was saying, I started to think about you and your warning to me. That night, the business associate I was supposed to meet called to confirm I was going. I became suspicious of what was going to happen, so I sent one of my other men down there, and . . ." he stops talking and shrugs his shoulders.

"He was killed instead of you?" I ask, completely horrified.

"He understood the dangers of the job."

"You sent someone else down there, and he was killed because you didn't go?" I head over to the bed, and sit on the edge. I stopped one man getting killed, but he sent someone else who took his place.

"He understood the d . . ."

"Bullshit!" I stand and shout at him. "Bullshit. You gutless piece of shit. You sent someone else who died. I saved you, and you sent someone else to die. You could've saved him, you could've . . ."

"I had to see if it was an ambush, like you said it was. And it turned out, you were right."

"Of course, I was right, you idiot. Why do you think I would've warned you if I wasn't right?"

"Here's the problem I had after my employee was killed." I cringe at the mere word of 'killed,' especially considering it could've been avoided. "The problem I had was, well . . . you."

"Me? Why am I problem?"

"Not are, but were."

I huff out a frustrated breath and shake my head. I'm on the brink of yelling at him again, but I have to stay focused and try to figure out what exactly happening, so I can get out of here. "Just tell me what's going on." My jaw clenches and I tighten my hand into a fist.

"How would you know I was going to the docks, considering you don't know who I am? I sat in my office for hours, trying to figure it all out. Trying to find a connection between you and me. Are you an associate's daughter, or possibly a mistress, or even maybe a wife to someone?"

"You do know I'm only sixteen?"

"Seventeen in a few days," he cockily replies.

The hair at the back of my neck stands to attention. This guy is super creepy and weirding me out.

Standing, I back away from him. How does he know my birthday is in a few days? What else does he know about me? "How . . . how do you know?" I clear my throat. My voice deceives the confidence I had, now I'm a shell of nervousness.

"I know your birthday is in four days. I know your mother is Judge Wren Murphy, and at the moment she's the sitting judge in a case where she's been threatened, and so have you."

"I have?" I ask. "That's why I have Marcus."

"I also know, your father, Clinton Murphy is her bailiff. I know the high school you go to. I know your best friend is Dallas Riley, who is a freak about the color purple."

My mouth opens, and I find it hard to speak. A strangled grumble escapes, but nothing more comes out.

"Would you like me to continue?"

It takes me a few moments to find the ability to speak again. He remains quiet, just keeping his eyes on me. "How did you find me?"

"The mall. I had my people hack into the surveillance, and I watched the moment your friend pushed you into me. I watched it over and over again. Do you know what intrigued me the most about that moment?" He waits for me to answer, but all I can do is shake my head. "She pushed you into me, I caught you so you wouldn't fall, and for the smallest amount of time, your eyes blanked. Like you weren't even there. It's not a long space of time, less than a few seconds, and not enough for someone to notice."

"But you did."

"Not to begin with. I watched the tape at least fifty times, if not more before I picked up on it."

"What exactly did you pick up?" Man, I'm feeling so vulnerable. I think he knows the secret I've been so desperate to hide.

"I noticed when I touched you, you went blank. You ran away, then you stopped and came to find me."

I move from foot to foot, uncomfortably. If he knows, how many other people know too? "And?"

"You have a gift, Lexi. Don't you?"

"Right now, it feels like a curse."

"You didn't answer my question. You have a gift." This time it's not a question. It's a definite statement. He's not asking, he's declaring what he knows. "And that makes you very, *very* special."

"How?"

He smiles at me, and shakes his head. "You have no idea the potential you hold."

"Potential?"

"You may see it as a gift, as do I. But others may see it as much more than that." I scrunch my brows at him. "Your gift has the potential to make you a weapon."

Ice covers my exposed skin and dread fills my lungs as I feel the blood drain from my face. My body shakes; my breath gets caught in the back of my throat.

A weapon.

"I'll never do anything to hurt anyone," I whisper. "Never."

With my back to the wall, I sink to the floor. I never thought of myself as anything more than just me, Alexa Murphy. I'm not a weapon, hell I don't even want to have this damn gift I've been given. "I don't know how I got it." I hug my knees and burst into tears. "I don't want to hurt anyone."

"I know you don't. But the fact is, someone will figure it out, like I did and they're going to want you to use you for their own personal gain."

"Is that why you took me? To use me?" I look up to find him still sitting on the bench seat beneath the window.

"You're useful to me, Lexi. Very useful, and I won't hurt you. But I will use you to benefit myself. And in return I promise to look after you."

A weapon.

Shocked, and frightened I sit on the floor cradling my legs. "I don't believe you. You're going to hurt me," I say adamantly.

"If you do what I want you to, then no, I won't hurt you."

"And if I don't cooperate with you?" I lift my head and arch my brow at him in defiance.

"You don't want to know the answer to that."

"So, you will hurt me?"

"I'll hurt everyone important to you, but no, you I won't touch. Because you'll have to live with the aftermath of refusing to help me."

I stare at him blankly. He's basically just said he'll hurt everyone I love and let me live with the consequences. As I'm staring at him, tears well in my eyes, and fall over. I suck back the sob so desperate to escape. Spit is gathering in my mouth while I stare at the man who now controls my future. "If I do what you want?" I ask trying to hold back my cries.

"Then everyone you love keeps breathing."

"You'd kill everyone to teach me a lesson?"

"In a heartbeat."

"You're . . . you're . . ."

"I'm a monster. But I always keep my word, and I swear on my life, I will never harm you."

"Because I'm too valuable to you."

"Yes," he answers candidly.

"And what if, whatever this thing I have goes away the way it came to me?"

His left eye slightly twitches and his lips thin into a straight line. "We'll revisit the conditions if it ever occurs."

"I could lie." I feel like slapping myself. Why would I say that to him?

"I'll figure it out, and I'll kill everyone. I figured out what you can do so far, and I'll figure out if you're lying, Lexi."

I keep staring at him. He really is a good-looking guy. He can't be any older than twenty-two or twenty-three, but I doubt his age has anything to do with his ruthlessness. "Get out," I say while staring at him. I want to smack him. I want to grab something and smash it against his fucking head. "GET OUT!"

He stands, buttons up his suit jacket and heads for the door. "I'll have food sent up to you in a few moments. Please, wear what you like, the wardrobe has been stocked in everything you may require. The bathroom has whatever you need, and there are towels in the storage cupboard in the bathroom. The housekeeper will be here in the morning. If you need anything, you can either look up there and ask." He points to the corner of the room, and I see a tiny camera pointing down. "Or you can knock on the door, and the guard stationed outside will call me."

"The door's locked. Why do I need a guard? Is it in case I break the window and jump out?"

"The window is unbreakable."

"Of course, it is." I roll my eyes at him.

"You have no allergies to any food, so my chef will make you something appropriate to eat."

"You might try to poison me."

He shakes his head and smiles. "You're too useful to me to poison you."

"I hate you." I stand from the floor and straighten my shoulders at him. "I hate you so much."

"I'm not the bad person here, Lexi. You'll eventually figure it out."

"Threatening to kill my parents and my best friend puts you at the top of the list of assholes who are in fact, bad people."

"I want to protect you, but I also want to use your gift."

"At this moment, it's nothing more than a curse. And I fucking hate you," I spit angrily toward him.

He gives me a curt nod, turns and leaves. The door closes with a resonating bang, and the finality of this situation dawns on me.

I'm stuck here, and if I don't do what he wants, he's going to kill everyone and let me live with the consequences.

And he says he's not the bad person.

What an asshole.

CHAPTER 11

I'VE BEEN STUCK in this room for a day. There's a huge, beautiful clock beside the door that continues to tick. It's driving me nuts, because it's the only sound I can hear.

True to his word, Jude has sent food up to me, but I haven't had an appetite. He's also sent a doctor in to see me and make sure I'm okay. The doctor was wearing gloves, so I suspect he's under instructions not to touch me.

I'm lying on the bed, and I'm staring up at the blank ceiling. There's a knock on the door, before I hear it unlock and open. I sit up, and watch as to who's going to come in.

Jude enters the room, and stands in the open doorway. "What do you want?" I ask.

"The chef said you haven't eaten anything he's sent up for you."

"Not hungry." I turn over in the bed and stare out the window.

"You have to eat, or you'll become weak."

"Not hungry."

"Well too bad. The chef is sending our lunch up, and you'll have to eat it."

Man, he's pissing me off. "And what if I'm not hungry? It's a bit difficult to eat when I've been told that I'm going to be your lackey or you'll kill my parents and best friend. You being an asshole and keeping me here against my will is not exactly conducive to a healthy appetite."

"I apologize if you think it's against your will. Please." He steps aside from the door and sweeps his hand to the open space.

"I can go?" I don't get him, he's up to something. He'll shoot me in the head the moment I step outside this bedroom.

"Don't let me stop you."

Standing from the bed, I slip my shoes on and take a step toward the door. There's the same guy standing on the other side, looking intimidating and scary. "But you're going to shoot me."

"I won't kill you, no."

I take another step. My heart's pounding and suddenly excitement fills me. "I can go?"

"Free as a bird." He steps further back. "But you won't have anyone to go to."

He's going to kill my parents and Dallas. "That's not a fucking choice. You're going to kill them."

"I said I would. But the choice is most certainly yours. The moment you leave the grounds of this house, the phone call will be made."

I step forward to him and slap his face as hard as I can. It stings my hand, but I don't care. I slap him again. He doesn't stop me. And I slap him a third time, then collapse to the floor in a mess. "Just let me go."

"You're free to go."

"But you'll kill my parents and Dallas."

"Yes. But the choice is yours."

"Then I'm not free. I'm not free to leave, I'm not free to live my life."

"You'll live your life here. With me."

"I hate you."

"I know."

"Why are you doing this?" I cover my face with my hands and cry into them. I hate him. I know the questions I'm asking are leading to an endless cycle of torture.

"Come on." He steps forward and grabs me by the elbow to help me up. I'm wearing a t-shirt and his skin on me, drags me into a vision.

"She's to be protected at all costs." He's standing in a room, in front of eight men all dressed in dark suits similar to his. I recognize the one standing outside my door, but none of the others.

I look around the room and try to find an exit point. The window in his office is opened, and a gust of air blows in, making a paper on the big, grand desk fly off.

"Bullshit," one of the men coughs-mumbles.

Jude's head swiftly turns to him, and makes his way over to the guy. "Do you have a problem?"

"This is babysitting duty. Who the hell is she?" the guy responds.

I see the anger in Jude's face. His jaw clenches and his eyes narrow. "Have you got a problem with the task I'm assigning you?"

"This is bullshit, Mr. Caley. She's locked up in that room, and she's not going anywhere, so why do I have to watch out for her? Why do any of us have to watch out for her?"

Jude straightens to his full height, and with all his might punches the guy in the nose. "I pay you, not the other way around. Next time you disrespect me, I put a bullet in your brain. You'll do what I tell you."

The guy is holding his nose, as blood is oozing out of it.

"You say . . ."

And I'm back in my room, on my feet, face to face with Jude. "What did you see?"

"It doesn't matter," I reply and step away from him.

"This isn't how it works, Lexi. I'm giving you the benefit of the doubt because this is new to you. But you're now in my world. And in my world, you tell me what you see."

I shake my head and walk away over to the bench seat. Sitting I let out a pained sigh. "You were in your office."

"And?" He sits on the bed opposite me.

"You were giving instructions to eight of your men."

"What type of instructions?"

"About me. You were telling them that I'm to be protected at any cost. One of them wasn't agreeing with you."

"Oh, is that right?" he asks, suddenly more invested in the vision. "And who was it?"

"I don't know, you didn't mention anyone by name. But the guy, he wasn't happy with you. You punched him and broke his nose."

"And?"

"That's as far as it went. I didn't see anything else before I was back here."

"And you saw all of that in the couple of seconds I was touching you?" I avoid his eyes, and nod. "What are you not telling me, Lexi?"

Asshole. "I looked around your office and saw your window open. It blew a sheet of paper off your desk."

"You know the rules. If you want to escape, then you can, but you understand the consequences."

"Then why do you lock me in here considering I really can't leave."

"You've made a fair point. I'll leave the room unlocked, but there'll always be someone outside your door."

I crinkle my nose and think about what he's said. If my door remains unlocked, that means others can get in, even when I'm asleep. "Who has a copy of the key to the door?" This is going to sound crazy, but I'll feel safer if the door remains locked. Jude's done nothing yet to make me think he'll hurt me, and he's made it so obvious he has no intentions on hurting me, but it doesn't mean one of his 'guys' will have the same feelings toward a sixteen-year-old female.

"I do, the chef, the doctor, and the maid. But that camera is always on, and I have a direct feed wherever I am."

"And what if you're not here?"

"You'll be with me."

I think about the whole situation, and I'll feel safer — if that's the word — if I know the door's locked. "Can you keep it locked?"

"Don't trust yourself not to escape?"

"You really are an asshole. I know I won't leave, but I don't want to be sexually assaulted, or beaten because someone thinks protecting me is beneath them. Or they think I'm a cute sixteen-year-old, so why shouldn't they take something they're not entitled to."

"You're seventeen soon, and if any one of my men touched you, I'd kill them myself."

"I'm not an idiot, Jude. There's no such thing as loyalty among criminals. They'd all happily sell you out if they think they'll get ahead for themselves."

"Hmm, interesting you say this."

"Why?"

"Because if you're right, then you'll find something when you touch them all."

"You want me to touch how many people?"

"We'll start with my chef when he brings us our lunch."

"I'm not a trained monkey, I don't know how this works. I have no idea how often I can do it and not burn myself out. I can't perform on cue."

There's a knock on the door, and a guy wearing a checkered black and white apron brings in a cart with two silver domes on top of it. The guy is old, maybe in his sixties with no hair on his head with a salt and pepper moustache.

"Lunch, sir," he says to Jude.

"Thank you, please bring it here." Jude has got such nice manners, *for a cold-hearted bastard.*

Jude looks at me as the old guy wheels the cart over to us. He slightly jerks his head to the side, indicating I have to touch the chef.

"Thank you, the smell is amazing," I say when he lifts the silver dome on my side. I gently touch his hand and I'm in a vision.

The man is at home, in a quiet dining room, eating dinner on his own. I look around and notice a large black and white photo above the mantel. It's an older type of picture, with two incredibly young people posing in their wedding photo. It's definitely the chef, and a stunning blonde woman. They're both smiling at the camera. They look so happy.

The man has set a place beside him, though no one is sitting with him. I keep looking around, and I see a jar which I now realize is an urn on top of the mantel.

"I miss you, Janet," he whispers as he continues to eat.

He's so alone in this vision, but I can feel the loneliness radiating through to me.

"Thank you," Jude says as I'm thrust back into the room.

The chef smiles, and leaves, closing the door behind him.

Looking down at the plate of food, I focus on the chicken, mashed potato, and greens on the plate.

"What did you see?" Jude asks picking up his fork and starting to eat.

"He's lonely. His wife Janet passed away but he still sets a plate for her at dinner. They were married for a long time, and he misses her so much."

"Excellent. Now, eat." As much as I want to be on a hunger strike, the smell is making my stomach grumble with the need for food.

I search for my cutlery, and find a flimsy plastic fork, no knife. I pick up the fork and huff. "Are you kidding me?" I slam the stupid fork down.

"What?" Jude eats with his proper cutlery.

"You have got to be the biggest asshole I know. Plastic? You gave me a plastic fork, which won't even pierce the chicken, and no damn knife. You really are horrible."

"You may try to hurt yourself with cutlery."

"I'll hurt you before I hurt myself. But considering you're trying to rule my damn life, here, cut my food." I shove my plate toward him.

He moves my plate in front of him, and cuts my food. When he finishes, he slides the plate back in front of me.

"There you go."

"Will you be gracing me with your presence at every meal?" I sarcastically ask. "Just so I know if I should dress up."

He laughs. "You really have quite a lot of spunk. I like that about you, Lexi."

"I don't like you," I automatically retort.

"I'll be joining you as often as possible."

I lower my eyes and eat a couple of mouthfuls. "Great."

"Look at me," he demands.

I look up at him, and he moves his face forward. "I never noticed, but you have a green eye, and your other eye has vivid blue colorings."

I jump up off my seat, and run into the bathroom to look at my eye.

My left eye is bluer now than it was when Dallas pointed it out. "How is this happening?" I ask as I stare at myself.

Jude appears in the doorway, and leans against the jamb. "What is it?"

I shake my head, not wanting to tell him. He doesn't need to know, it's not a vision so it has nothing to do with him. "It doesn't matter." I step back, and move past him.

"Lexi." He grabs my upper arm where my t-shirt is covering my arm. "What is it?"

"It's not a vision, so it doesn't matter."

"But if it's got to do with you, then I need to know." He pushes away from the door frame and follows me back to where we were eating our food.

"Fine."

"Well?"

"My eye is changing color, and I haven't worked out why yet. They were both green, but this one started changing to blue." I point to my left eye.

"I'll have an optometrist come to see you," he casually says as he picks his fork up to continue eating.

"No, there's nothing wrong with my vision. It's the color that's changing."

"I'll have it checked out," he insists. "To make sure you're okay."

"I'm fine. I don't want to see an optometrist. There's nothing wrong with my eye except the color is changing."

"Okay, no optometrist."

Finally, something I won. Then it dawns on me, is he going to kill my parents? "Are you going to kill my mom or dad or Dallas because I said no eye doctor?" I hold my breath and wait for his answer.

"No, why would I?"

I drop my fake fork on the plate of food. "You're so frustrating, Jude. You scare the shit out of me and tell me you'll kill everyone I love if I try to leave, but then you sit there and look amused that I think you'll kill them because I'm refusing the eye doctor."

"My rule is I will kill them if you leave. Not if you refuse the optometrist."

And just like that, my appetite is gone, again.

I stand and make my way over to the door which I open. "Can you leave? And take the food with you."

He picks up his real cutlery, and steps away from the cart. "I'll leave the food, but I'm taking the cutlery."

"And I'll eat it with my stupid plastic fork. Just take the whole damn thing."

"Then eat it with your hands." He slams the door shut, and I hear the door locking.

What an asshole to the hundredth degree.

CHAPTER 12

HAPPY-FREAKING-BIRTHDAY to me.

Seventeen and stuck in a room with four walls and nothing to do.

Great.

As I lie on the bed, staring up at the blank ceiling, the door unlocks and the guy who I saw in the vision comes into the room. His nose is inflamed and he has dark bruises ringing his eyes. "Boss wants you," he curtly says to me.

"I don't care what he wants. He can come and tell me himself." I continue to lie on the bed, not jumping to the demands of Jude.

"Get up," he says in an eerily controlled voice.

"No. I'm not going anywhere with you."

"Get the fuck up, you spoiled little bitch. I don't give a fuck if you're sleeping with the boss or not, you're a damn thorn in my side." He storms over to the bed and grabs me by the hair, yanking me off the mattress.

I land on the floor with a huge thwack, hitting my back against the edge of the bed. Screaming out in pain, I try and find traction, but the huge guy drags me by my hair toward the door. "Let me go!" I scream at him.

He swings around and drags me up by my hair. With as much force as he's got, he backhands my cheek. My head swings to the right and an earth-shattering pain rips through my face. "Help," I yell loudly, hoping the guy outside my door is there and can help me.

"No one here to help you, *pet.*"

He grabs a handful of my hair and drags me further out of the room. Crying, and in pain, I'm being tossed around like a rag doll.

He pulls me out of the room, and I try to look around me, but he's being so rough with me that all I can do is grab onto my head and hope he doesn't rip my hair out from the roots.

We get to the top of a staircase and he lets me go. I take this opportunity to run down the stairs, hoping I don't fall and kill myself.

I get to the bottom step and leap off it, running toward the front door. The guy standing in front of it looks just as menacing as the guy who came into my room.

"You can't leave," he says in a monotone.

Hysterically I beat against him, trying to get away from the guy who's roughing me up. The guy at the door, lifts his hand and talks into the cuff of his shirt. "Get the boss here, now."

The guy who beat me casually stops at the bottom of the stairs and places his hands on his hips looking at me.

Jude comes into the foyer and looks at me hiding behind the huge guy at the door. He looks at me, and then at the guy with a busted nose. "What happened?" he asks the guy.

"I went into her room, like you told me, and she screamed and launched herself at me. I pushed her off me, and she slammed her head into the side of the wall. Sorry, Boss, but she attacked me."

"Bullshit," I yell. "That's not what happened, and you know it. You grabbed my hair and dragged me off the bed."

He rolls his eyes at me and shoves his hands in his pockets. "Yeah, 'cause I don't value my life after this." He points to his nose then shoves his hand back into his pocket.

Jude looks to me, his eyes squinting. "Come here, Lexi."

Meekly I shuffle forward to stand in front of Jude. He grabs my chin and moves my face so he assess me for himself.

I'm in a vision. Jude's sitting in his office looking over a stack of paperwork. He's massaging his temple with his left hand as he lets out an exasperated sigh. His cell phone rings beside him, he stops what he's doing and picks his phone up.

"Yeah," he answers the phone in a dead serious tone.

I lean in to listen to the conversation. Closing my eyes, I focus on the phone call. I use all my energy to try and hear the other person. " . . . done." Is all I hear.

"Good." Jude ends the call and tosses his phone on the huge desk. He leans back in his chair and runs his hand over his face, then his hair.

Standing in his office I watch him, and his reaction to the phone call. A small smile pulls at his lips, and he looks up at the ceiling to his right. "I told you, I'll always look after you." He keeps looking up for a few seconds, before moving his chair forward and going back to his work.

"This most certainly looks like a run in with a wall," Jude says while studying my face. And I'm back to the now.

"Yeah, that's what I said, Boss." He cockily smirks at me, and I want to smash his head in.

"Only one problem," Jude 'tsks' as he turns to look at Mr. Cocky.

"What's that?"

"I have a video feed from her room, and I know exactly what happened." Out of nowhere, four heavily armed men appear. They surround the cocky guy and wait. Jude lifts his hand and flicks it toward them. "You know what to do," he says. With his hand to my back, he turns us around and leads me away from the foyer.

"What are you going to do?" I ask as I look over my shoulder to see the men dragging Mr. Now-Not-So-Cocky away.

"He was warned." He doesn't answer the question, but at the same time he tells me enough for me to piece it all together.

"Jude, no!" I stop walking and grab onto his covered arm. "You can't kill him."

"I'm not going to kill him," he responds with a smirk.

"I thought . . ." I shake my head and take a deep breath. "I thought you were going to kill him."

Jude smiles at me and leads me toward the direction he wants me to go. "No, *I'm* not going to kill him."

It dawns on me, and I sigh with hurt. I stop walking and look up into his dark eyes. I pay particular attention, because they're so dark, I'd say they're black, and I've never seen black eyes before. "I don't want to be responsible for his death. Please, don't," I plead with Jude.

"You have nothing to do with what will happen to him."

"Jude," I huff with irritation. "Knowing it's because he did this . . ." I point to the side of my throbbing face, " . . . means I'm responsible for his death."

"Did you ask him to open his hand so you could run, face first, into it?"

"Well . . . no, that's ridiculous."

"Did you ask him to drag you out of your room by your hair?" I shudder and look away from Jude, opting to not answer.

"Why did he do that? Is that how people like you treat women?"

"People like me?" He again starts in the direction he wants to take me. "What does that even mean?"

"Who are you trying to kid? You kidnapped me, without any remorse. You've threatened everyone I love, again without any remorse. But that guy smacks me around, and you give an order to, I don't know . . . hurt or kill him." The heaviness sits on my chest. I'm part of something I don't want to be a part of, but I'm here and I have to live with whatever is going to happen to me. Or I have to live with the consequences. I look around because it feels like we've been walking for half an hour, even though I know it's only been a few moments. "Where are we going?" I stop walking, looking around me.

"This way." He gestures toward an opening at the back of the house.

This place is beyond massive. It's like a mansion on steroids. "Do you live here alone?" I ask as we head out to what is a huge, open kitchen.

"No, I live here with you."

I squint my eyes at him and shake my head. "It's not what I meant. How many people live here?"

He gestures to a large wooden table, big enough to seat at least twenty people. At the head of the table, there's a cake with one candle burning in the middle of it. "Happy birthday, Alexa." He touches the curve of my back and pushes me forward slightly.

"You got me a cake?" I turn to look at him, both his eyes, and his mouth are smiling. "Is it poisoned?"

He lets out a full belly laugh. "Make a wish, and I'll eat the first piece."

"Making a wish is redundant at this point in time, don't you think?"

"Wishing is free."

"But I'm not."

"You're as free as you can be," he says solemnly.

I lean over and blow out the candle. "I want to see my mom and dad again, Jude."

"I can't allow you do that."

A tear falls from my eye, and I quickly wipe it away so he doesn't see that he's made me cry. "I hate you so much," I manage to whisper through a controlled sob.

"Eat some cake." He pushes the cake toward me.

I look him straight in the eyes and straighten my shoulders. "You're pretending to be a decent guy, but there's nothing good about you."

He bites on the inside of his cheek before he replies with, "I know who I am, Lexi, I'm death. And you're my sickle until I no longer need you." My body wants to buckle under his cold words. "Make no mistake at all. I am and always will be darkness. I'm going to do everything in my power to use you, but not to ruin you. You should never be in my world, but you are. And you're in my world because of what you can do, not because of who you are."

I have nothing to say. He's just said in no uncertain words, I will be his weapon for as long as he wants me to be. "I can't do this, Jude. I can't be here." The tears start to well again and I'm seconds away from losing it in front of him. "Please, let me see my parents. I'll tell them I'm okay. They'll be going crazy trying to find me. Please?"

He shakes his head, and sticks his hands in his suit pants. "No."

"Please?" I shamelessly beg. "I'll tell them I've met someone and I'm moving in with them?"

He takes a deep breath, and offers me a sympathetic smile. A smile that speaks volumes. The words are loud even though nothing is being said. I know the answer, and I don't even need to hear it.

"Please?" I beg again.

He drags a chair out and sits down. "Have some cake." He moves it closer to me again.

My veins pulsate with anger, and my heart snaps with sadness. Is it possible to have a broken heart and be seething with rage in the same heartbeat? Well I fucking am.

"Screw your stupid cake." I pick it up and throw it at him. "Let me see my parents."

Jude doesn't even flinch, he simply sits in the chair, wearing the cake. He dips his finger through the frosting and licks it. If he wasn't an asshole, and if he wasn't keeping me hostage, then watching him lick his finger may have been strangely erotic. But, the fact is, he *is* an asshole, and he *is* keeping me against my will.

"You can go anywhere on the property you like. If the room is locked, you're to stay out of it. The moment your feet are off the property, I'll make the phone call."

"I just want to see them," I scream in his face.

"Anywhere you want to go, you can." He stands from the seat, and the cake falls to the floor. "One step off my land and you know what will happen."

From his chest to his knees, he's covered in cake. "Just let me go." In a futile attempt at getting through to him, I cry and stomp my foot. I can only imagine how I look, but I really don't care. I just want to see my parents.

"Happy birthday, Alexa. I have a special dinner planned for you tonight. Please join me in the foyer at six." He's talking to me like I *want* to live here, like I *want* to be part of all of this.

"No, I won't. Just let me go home."

"I'm going to change then I'll be in my office if you require anything."

He steps away and leaves me crying in the dining room. Sinking to the floor, I gather myself into a ball and sob. This is seriously screwed.

When my tears finally stop, I look up and out through the back glass sliding doors. The entire kitchen wall is glass and overlooking a mammoth pool. Beyond the pool is acres and acres of superbly manicured, thick, green grass.

Jude has made it clear to me. Crystal clear. I leave, he'll kill my parents and best friend. I stay, they'll live.

He says I have a choice, but we both know, I don't.

CHAPTER 13

I DIDN'T FEEL like a special celebratory dinner last night, so when Jude sent for me, I told the new thug I wasn't feeling well.

Jude left me alone.

He knew the truth, even though I didn't say it to him.

I wanted to spend my birthday with my parents and Dallas. Not Jude. He isn't my best friend or anything special to me.

The sun has broken through the window and is slowly getting higher in the sky. Lying in bed, I stare at the beauty of nature but feel like I could burst into tears. This is such a screwed-up situation.

Jude is treating me well, *for a caged animal.*

Caged in the way that there are dire consequences attached to me leaving.

I feel so helpless. So alone.

The door unlocks and swings open. I don't even care enough to see who enters the room. It could be Satan himself come to take me to the depths of hell, and I wouldn't care.

"Lexi, how are you today? I missed you at dinner last night." Jude sits on the end of my bed and stares at me.

"Wasn't hungry," is my only response as I continue to gaze outside.

"Are your living arrangements satisfactory for you?"

I look over at him and roll my eyes. "Seriously? And what would you do if they weren't? Let me go?" Turning my head again, I stare outside.

"I'd like to make it as comfortable as possible for you."

"Jude, what do you want? We're going around in endless circles here. I want out, you want to pretend to be nice so you don't scare me but you won't let me go, because I'm too valuable to you. Which brings me back to my original question, what do you want?" He lifts his eyebrow at me, and smirks. "When you do that," I point to his face. " . . . I wanna smash your head in."

He chuckles at me, which makes me even madder. "Well then, I'll cut to the chase. You'll be accompanying me to dinner tonight."

"And the purpose of this dinner?" I'm not an idiot, I know he wants to use me.

"I need you to touch a man named Alfred and tell me what you see."

"And how much of a choice do I have in this?" I stare into his dark and dangerous eyes.

"As much as you want. You always have the choice to say no." He takes his phone out of his pocket and slides his finger across the screen.

I know what he's doing. The tears prickle my eyes, but I hold them in. I push the hate as far down as I can, cornering it in a part of me that will keep it at bay. "You're a pig." I turn my back on him.

"I'd be delighted if you could join me tonight. I'll have appropriate clothing sent up to your room."

I feel the bed move and know he's leaving. "I shouldn't have come after you to tell you about the dock."

"You'll learn that I may be cloaked in darkness, but with you, I'll only give you my light."

"You're a walking, talking, sack of contradicting shit. You'll only give me your light, but you're more than prepared to give the order to kill everyone I love. There's no light in you, Jude.

Your flame has been extinguished by your black heart." He's still in my room. "I'll be ready when you want me to be."

"Be downstairs by eight. The appropriate attire will be sent to you. If I'm missing something, please let me know."

"You're missing a soul."

He clears his throat, and then I hear the door latch closed. Closing my eyes, I try and go back to sleep. I hate this life I'm living, if that's what it can be called.

Washing my hair in the shower, I hear someone come into the bedroom. Panic should quickly rise, but it doesn't. I know, if any of these men wanted to hurt me, they would've done it already. And the one man who did hurt me isn't breathing any more.

It's stupid, I should be worried about my safety, but strangely, my brain has decided to accept that as long as I'm here Jude will make sure I'm safe.

Don't get me wrong, I still don't want to be here, and I am, in fact imprisoned. I want to go home, and I want to see my parents, but I know that will never be possible.

Dragging myself out of the shower, I wrap a towel around my body and one around my hair and head into the bedroom.

On the bed is a huge white box with a vibrant blue ribbon wrapped around, and a small white box with no ribbon.

Seriously, dude, this isn't a date.

Untying the ribbon, I open the box and find a green evening gown. I should be excited about the beautiful dress, but I'm not. I have to look at this situation as work. He's paying, in the form of not killing the people I love. In return, I provide a service.

I lift the dress out of the tissue paper it's wrapped in and look it over. There's no denying it, the dress is gorgeous. It's long and fitted, and has sheer, nearly transparent chiffon sleeves. Whoever selected this chose wisely, because it's something I'd pick for myself.

I drape the pretty dress down over the box it came in, and open the other. It has a pair of gold, strappy heels. Again, beautiful and something I'd pick for myself. The heels aren't too high, but enough to add some height to my nearly five foot eight frame.

Swinging one of the shoes around on my pinkie, I toss it on the bed. "You know, Jude, you're quite disturbing. You know my size, and you have good taste. The disturbing part is you know these things." I smile to myself, and know he's listening and watching me. "I'll bet you're gay. Gay men always have great fashion sense."

I walk into the bathroom, and drop my towel at the door. No use in modesty, I bet the sick bastard has a camera in here too.

It doesn't take me long to blow dry my hair and straighten it, and to apply a thin layer of makeup. I'm not doing this for him, I'm doing it because I've decided I'm going to treat it like employment, where the currency traded is my services for my parents' and best friend's lives.

I'm going to work.

Getting ready, and going to work. That's exactly what this arrangement is. Me working for him.

Naked, I head into the bedroom and put on underwear *he* bought for me. When I'm ready, I slip on the dress. It's beyond gorgeous, and the long chiffon sleeves end in a V with a thin piece of elastic wrapping around my middle finger to keep it in place.

Sitting on the bed, I slip my feet into the pretty shoes, buckle the straps, and stand. Other than the medicine cabinet mirror in the bathroom, there's nothing here I can see myself in.

There's a knock on the door, and the regular meathead comes in. "Miss Murphy, the boss is waiting for you downstairs," he blankly says.

"Considering I'm going to be living here for who knows how long, can you at least tell me your name?"

He crosses his arms over in front of his chest and plants his feet hip width apart. "The boss is waiting."

Rolling my eyes, I walk past him. I want to shoulder-butt him, but he's built like he's a tank, and I'd more likely hurt myself than him.

Heading out of the room, I walk along the hallway and down the grand staircase. Jude is dressed in a tuxedo; his jet-black hair is styled to the side. He impatiently looks at his watch then turns to search for me.

I'm half-way down the stairs when he notices me, his eyes widen and his lips pull up into a smirk. "Wow, you look absolutely stunning," he says. His eyes travel the length of my body, taking in the dress he bought.

A small, stupid-ass flutter trembles in my stomach. I've never had a man look at me the way he is right now. Although completely flattering, I know the truth behind his handsome appearance and dark and dangerous eyes. "Thanks," I reply curtly. "You look alright too."

"You'll definitely be the one who'll have all the attention."

"Great, attention, exactly what I crave," I say sarcastically.

He places his hand to the small of my back, and leads me to the front door. "Wait, where are your gloves?" he asks stopping by the front door.

"Gloves? There weren't any in the box. Anyway, I can't wear gloves with this dress. It wouldn't go."

"You have to wear them, so when you shake people's hands, you don't get a vision until you meet Alfred."

"Jude, gloves don't go with this dress. I'm not wearing them. Easy solution to this, I won't shake anyone's hand. Anyway, how are you going to introduce me? Oh, this is the girl I've kidnapped and keeping against her will?"

"You're my girlfriend. Now go and get the gloves."

"Your *what*? Are you serious?"

"Yes, get the gloves. I don't want anyone even getting a slight indication of what you're capable of." He stands firm inside the door.

"You really want me to wear those stupid gloves that won't go with this outfit?"

"Yes."

"Then you go and get them. I'll be waiting for you in the car." The guy standing at the front door smirks at me as I walk toward him. He stands there, like a brick wall and doesn't move. "Get out of my way." He looks to Jude, who I hear chuckle from behind me. "Don't look at him. I told you to move." He looks again to Jude, and this pisses me off even more.

"Move," Jude instructs the guy at the door.

He steps aside and opens the front door for me. I narrow my eyes at him as I walk past him. The moment I'm outside, I'm hit with the distinctive aroma of jasmine flowers. Closing my eyes, I inhale deeply and take in the sweet aroma. "Jasmine this time of the year?" I ask myself as I look around the front of the ridiculously huge mansion. The walls aren't stucco or brick, they're huge sandstone boulders. As I step further out, I take in the magnificence and opulence of this place. "Wow," I whisper as I look up to see the house towering proudly on the picturesque acreage.

The sun is setting in the far distance, but it looks close enough that if I reach out I can touch it. It'll be dark within moments, but the colors in the sky are majestic.

The breathtaking sky doesn't stop my heart hurting, and my curiosity piquing. My heart is aching because I'll never see my parents again, and my curiosity is piqued because I have no idea where the hell Jude is taking me tonight. One thing I do know, I'm here to work for Jude and that's all.

CHAPTER 14

A LONG BLACK limousine pulls up in front of the house, and the driver, dressed identically to all the other men who work for Jude, gets out and comes to open the back door. "Miss Murphy," he states as he looks ahead and not at me.

I slide into the back, and within a couple of minutes Jude joins me. "Here," he says and hands me the ugliest looking lacey gloves I've ever seen.

"Oh, no way am I wearing those! No way." I turn my head to look out the window.

"Wear the damn gloves, Lexi."

"No. You somehow managed to pick a gorgeous dress, and pretty shoes, and the ugliest gloves I've ever laid eyes on. Don't even think I'm putting those on my hands. They don't even go with the dress."

The car rolls out of the long driveway and both of us are completely silent in the car. I look forward, staring at the back of the driver's head. The partition slowly rises and I grumble internally.

"Wear the damn gloves." Jude thrusts them toward me.

"No." I turn my head and look out at the scenery.

"Wear the damn gloves, Lexi!" he booms.

His loud, rumbly voice instantly makes me flinch in my seat. I move further away from him and grasp at the door handle, ready for what's to come.

Closing my eyes I wait for the strike. I've made him angry, and this frightens me.

Shut up, Lexi and do what he wants you to do. Your parents' lives are on the line.

"You're shivering," he says from beside me. "Here." I turn to look at him, frightened. He leans forward, takes off his tuxedo jacket and holds it out to me. I eye the jacket, then my gaze travels back to him in question. "You're cold." He angles sideways and tries to throw his jacket over my shoulders.

"I'm okay," I reply in a small, meek voice.

"For someone who has a smart mouth, you obviously can't take what you dish out."

Swallowing the dread constricting my throat, I scrunch my brows together. "I can take it, I just can't handle the fear."

"What are you scared of?" Again, he tries to drape his jacket around my shoulders.

"Jude, do we have to go over this again? You're keeping me here against my will." He goes to open his mouth but I hold my hand up at him, halting him from speaking further. "I know what you're going to say, but really, no matter how you word it, I'm here against my will. That frightens me. You frighten me. You yelling at me scares me."

"I'll never do anything to hurt you."

This guy really doesn't get it. "You may not hurt me, but I know what you're capable of. One day, you may not like what I say or see . . ." I point to my eyes and refer to the visions I get, " . . . and you may retaliate against me. I don't want to be here. But I am, because my family means more to me than I mean to me."

His hard eyes soften, and this is the first time since he's had me, that I think I'm getting through to him. He looks away from me, unable to meet my eyes. I can tell he's thinking about this and how wrong it is, although, he also doesn't strike me as the type of guy who cares about wrong or right. No quicker does he turn back, he puffs his chest out and lifts his chin. "You may not want to be here, but you are. So, wear the goddamn gloves." He lifts them from the space between us on the bench and thrusts them toward me again. "Now," he adds in the most eerie and deadpan voice.

I reach over and take them, sliding them on my hands. I turn back to watch the outside, wishing for the day to come where I'll be free from Jude and his reign of fear.

"Thank you," I hear him say in the smallest and quietest of voices. Swinging my head back, I try and get a look at his face, but he's turned. The only thing I can see is his reflection in the window, and his ordinarily hard features appear troubled.

"What do I have to do tonight?" I ask trying to change my own mood.

"Alfred is a business associate, I need you to shake his hand and tell me what you see."

"You know I'm not sure how this thing works, right?"

"Just tell me what you see."

"And if I see nothing?"

"Then tell me." He smiles at me, obviously aware of the crazy feelings running through me. I don't want him to think I'm lying to him if I don't see anything, because I don't want my parents to die. "Whatever you see." He reaches out and gently places his hand on my leg. When I look down, he quickly pulls back and shakes his head. "I apologize."

Letting out a deep sigh, I turn to study him. "You don't act like a . . . you know, to me."

Amused, his lips perk up into a smile. "A 'you know'?" he questions. "What's a 'you know'?" He air quotes.

Grumbling, I tilt my head to the side. "You know?" I say again. "One of you people."

"Now I'm a 'you people,' please clarify. Oh, and I'm completely amused by this exchange." He gestures between us.

"Don't be a jerk. You know what I mean."

"Please, don't let me stop you. I really want to know what it is I am. Continue." He leans forward, takes a glass, and pours some amber liquid from a decanter into it. The mini bar is stocked well, with a ton of medium sized alcoholic beverages in decanters. "I'd offer you a drink, however it's illegal for a seventeen-year-old to consume alcohol."

"Seriously?" I spit toward him. "You're worried it's illegal for me to drink?"

He swings his head around with a cheeky grin, "I was being sarcastic."

"More like idiotic," I mumble and quickly bring my hand up to my mouth realizing I said it aloud. "Shit."

He rumbles with laughter before throwing the amber liquid down his throat in one smooth movement. "Please, you were saying what people like me do."

"You know what it is. We all know what it is." I point to the driver who's unable to hear us due to the privacy screen.

"Come on, Lexi. I want to hear you say it."

"No."

"I think there'd be something quite sexy in saying the word."

My skin pebbles with excitement, and my stomach does this crazy flip when the word *sexy* rolls off his tongue. His dark eyes look straight through me as if he can read my mind. One minute he has me shivering with fear, the next I'm trembling with excitement. *Damn it, Lexi, get it together.*

"I'm not saying it. And we both know exactly who you are and what you do," I defiantly add. He smiles at me again, and the stupid effect his contagious smile has on me, makes me scold myself. *Again.*

"Okay, you don't have to say it." He chuckles. *Damn him.*

"Considering I'm stuck here with you, and considering the chances of me ever leaving are incredibly low, you may as well tell me about yourself."

Jude lets out a laugh, throwing his head back as the sound of amusement erupts in the car. "You want me to tell you about myself?"

"Did I just open Pandora's box? Should I ask Scotty to beam me up?"

"You know Star Trek?"

"Oh please. Dad is a Trekkie, and I was always forced to watch it. Live long and prosper." Bringing my hand up, I group my first two fingers, and last two fingers together.

"You constantly surprise me, Lexi. Constantly." His chuckle quickly dies down and he focuses on a spot on the bench seat. "I'm who I am because of my upbringing."

"I know nothing about you, Jude. Except for what I've seen on the television."

He steeples his fingers together and taps on his chin. "My father was in the business," he starts but doesn't clarify what 'the business' is. No need to, I'm no idiot. "He was killed in front of my eyes. My mother was then raped and tortured by the people who killed my father."

"Oh shit," I say, bringing my hand up to rest on my heart. "Why?"

Jude is lost in his own head, he has no idea I'm even here. The anger on his face tells a story, something quite sinister. "He refused to trade in children," he says in an almost casual voice. "He didn't want to be part of it. So, they killed him. They wanted more and more from him. He was a bad man, a cold-hearted killer. Anyone who'd cross him, he'd put down without asking questions. But when the people he was working for wanted him to trade in kids, he wouldn't do it. He refused it. He'd argue with them at meetings, and they didn't like it."

I want to reach out and touch him, give him a small amount of comfort, but I can't. I can't bring myself to give comfort to the man who'll kill the ones I love if I leave. "And what happened?"

Jude is still consumed by his own thoughts. His eyes are focused on a spot. "I watched them kill my parents. I watched what they did to them, and I vowed to hurt them more than they'd hurt me. Much more." He blinks and slowly turns his head to seek my eyes. My body shudders with fear. Jude easily invokes panic from deep within. The look in his eyes tell me that he's capable of inflicting horror. Horror I don't ever want to experience.

"You don't have to tell me any more."

I don't want to know anything else.

"Over time I integrated easily, and I took them out. Slowly and painfully. I made them bleed. I made them hurt." He chuckles at the obviously gruesome memory he has.

My chest constricts as a terrifying chill rips through my body. Jude's not telling me this to scare me, although he is. He's telling me what he's capable of. "There's not a doubt in my mind, you made them hurt." Not one iota of doubt.

He takes a deep breath making his chest puff out, then contract. He lets out a humorless laugh. His face is hard, his jaw rigid with anger, though it's not directed at me. His eyes though, they don't hold anger, they're full of hurt. "I showed them what torture really felt like, Lexi."

I swallow the lump in my throat, and hold my breath. How the hell do I respond? What do I say? I say nothing.

Turning my head away from him, I look out the window and remain quiet. The circumstances were horrible, but I can't agree with his actions. However, this does now make me see his situation differently. Clearly, he was born into a family where his father was involved with crime. It's the age old saying: monkey see, monkey do. Would Jude be different if he was born into a family of law-abiding citizens as opposed to a family of criminals?

I push the thoughts to the tiny compartment at the back of my mind. One where I really shouldn't think like this, because, Jude has kidnapped me and told me he'll kill everyone if I leave. I can't allow myself to feel sorry for him; he's not a good guy.

We pull up to a beautiful, opulent house. The style is more modern then Jude's but it's just as ostentatious. I already know the wealth amassed here has been acquired through illegal activity.

"You're my girlfriend," Jude announces as he opens the door to the limousine. "And therefore, I'll be treating you like I would my girlfriend."

Huh? "What does that even mean?" I ask before he exists the car.

"It means I'll be touching you and kissing you." I scowl while lifting my brows at him. "And it means you're going to put on a show and pretend to be in love with me." I scrunch my nose. He catches my reaction and laughs. "I don't want them to know who you are. To be precise, I don't want them to know what you're capable of, so you'll keep your gloves on until I introduce you to Alfred, then you'll remove your gloves and shake his hand."

"Ugh, fine." I'm a damn show pony, and I hate it.

"And one more thing, you're not to go anywhere, including the bathroom without one of my men with you. Do you understand?"

Seriously? I nod my head. "Yeah."

"It's for your safety. You're gorgeous, young, look incredible in that dress, and I can guarantee there'll be men here who'd love to push you up against a wall and have their way with you."

Bile quickly ascends to the back of my throat. "Lovely people you associate with."

"I'm sure half the women would love to have a piece of you too."

"Really? Just . . . stop." Not that I have a problem with homosexual or bisexual people, but I'm not interested. "I'm here to work," I say.

Jude smiles, and leaves the car. My door opens, and a guy dressed in black holds his hand out to me. Extending my hand, I reach out to grab it but he's quickly shoved away and Jude's in his place. "You don't touch her, ever," he growls toward his own guy.

"I'm sorry, Boss, I meant nothing by it," the guy quickly

replies.

Jude holds his gaze, the menacing stare he's giving his guy sends shocks through me. "Step away," Jude barks.

The guy steps back holding his hands up. Jude turns to face me, his features now softer and calmer. "Thank you," I say as I grab hold of his hand to help me out.

"My pleasure." Once I'm out, he links our arms together and walks toward the front door.

Another guy in black is standing at the entrance, marking people off as they enter. "Mr. Caley, welcome." He doesn't even make eye contact with me, and Jude completely ignores him.

If I didn't know the type of person Jude is, I'd think this fancy black-tie affair is above board and legal. "What's happening here?" I ask Jude as we walk into a beautiful, marble foyer.

"It's a charity event."

A laugh rips through me, and Jude sideways glares at me. "What's funny?"

"What's the event for?"

"To raise money for a half-way house for women who're transitioning from drugs."

I laugh again which earns me an eyebrow lift and a scowl. "Oh, come on, you can't see the irony in this?" I whisper to him as he leads me to the left into a massive ballroom filled with beautiful people.

He shrugs his shoulders nonchalantly at me. "I don't force anyone to buy drugs."

"How idiotic." Suddenly sadness overtakes me. This is the type of event my parents would have gone to. A small spark of hope filters through me, maybe I'll see them here. I already know the earth-shattering answer to my hopeful question. *No*, Jude wouldn't bring me somewhere I'd possibly see my parents.

"Champagne?" Jude offers when a waiter walks past us. He grabs two and holds it out to me.

"You want me to work, Jude. So . . . no."

He lifts his shoulders, drinks one of the flutes in a fluid motion and leaves both glasses on the edge of a small table already filled with empty glasses. He looks around the room, nods his head curtly toward a group of men on the other side. "The fat guy," he says to me as he leans in and whispers into my ear.

I look over his shoulder and see a short man, staring at me. He's very rotund, with beady eyes that are glued to me, and he's wearing pants that are way too short, ending above his ankles. "For someone who has money, you'd think his trousers would fit better."

Jude leans in even further, his cheek brushing against mine. Closing my eyes, I'm dragged into a vision. He's pacing in his office, running his left hand through his hair while his right hand is to his ear, listening to whoever he's speaking with on the phone.

He's stressed and worried.

I'm back in the ballroom, and Jude's pulled away while his eyes are focused on me. "What did you see?"

"You were in your office, and you looked concerned. It was just a glimpse, nothing in depth."

He turns his head and looks around us. His body becomes rigid and he lifts his chin with authority. "Alfred is on his way over."

Blinking quickly, I center my attention to the now. Taking my gloves off, I hold them in my left hand, ready to work.

"Jude, it's good to see you," the short, fat guy with ill-fitting pants says. His eyes are trained on me; he's not looking at Jude at all. "Who's this ravishing young lady?"

God, he's so sleazy. I watch as his gaze travels the length of my body, making me feel disgusting and dirty. *I think I threw up in my mouth.*

"Alfred, please meet my girl, Alexa."

"Alexa, such a beautiful name for a delicious-looking woman." He holds his hand out.

"Don't go getting any ideas. I'm keeping this one." Jude turns to me, and winks.

"I won't steal her, but if she wants a real man, she can always come to me."

His voice makes my skin crawl, and his words makes me want to projectile vomit all over him. "Obviously, you're referring to Jude." I can't help but look him up and down.

Alfred's face falters, though he quickly regains his composure. "Alfred," he thrusts his hand out to me, but I can see he's quite angry.

Taking his hand in mine, I'm instantly transported into a shabby office. I'm standing with the edge of his desk behind me and I look around the room. It's messy and dimly lit. There's a knock on the door, and Alfred tells whoever it is to come in. A younger man opens the door. He's got greasy, slicked-back hair, and he's chewing gum.

"Sit." Alfred gestures for the guy to enter. Immediately I notice the severe limp.

"It's all set up," Limpy says, sitting opposite Alfred and crossing one leg over the other. He settles back into the seat, relaxing like he belongs.

I turn to search Alfred's desk, but I see nothing of value except stacks of papers hopelessly strewn across his desk. They look more like trash than anything important.

"Good," Alfred replies.

"What about Caley?"

Alfred's lips turn up into a snide smile. Smugness envelops him as he leans back in his chair and places his chubby hands under his chin. "Fuck him. He doesn't need to know."

I turn back to look at Limpy. He obviously thinks Jude should know. "You sure about this?"

Alfred's laugh is loud and almost menacing. "I'll take care of him."

"Alfre-."

I'm ripped away before I catch any more of the conversation.

"I'm sure we'll meet again soon, my beautiful Alexa." Alfred walks away, and I'm left dazed and confused.

"Are you okay?" Jude asks.

"Give me a minute." I'm not sure why, but this vision has drained me. I grab onto his bicep and steady myself as I try and regain my composure.

"Do you need the bathroom?" Jude asks, worried. Nodding my head, he leads me down a hallway and opens the door to an exquisite bathroom. The faucets are gold, there's gold trim around the huge mirror, and there's marble lining the floors and walls.

Jude leads me in, and locks the door behind us. This room is huge, a luxurious powder room like something you'd see in a movie where all the characters were rich and famous.

Noticing a plush chair in front of the mirrored vanity, I head over and sit. Dropping my head in my hands, I take several breaths to regain myself.

"Are you okay?"

"I'll be fine," I snap at him. Is he asking because he cares, or is he asking because if I become useless to him, he doesn't have the advantage of my gift?

"Hey," he says in a gentler voice. He starts rubbing circles on my back, and although I welcome the touch—even through the fabric – I know he's only showing me this side of himself because he needs me.

"Please don't touch me." Looking into the mirror, I notice my eye. It's bluer than before. It seems to be changing when I have visions. "Alfred was sitting in a disgusting office, dirty and messy. A guy walked in and said 'it' was set. The guy who was with Alfred had a limp. He asked about you and Alfred said he'll take care of you."

I look at Jude in the reflection of the mirror. His brows are drawn together as he stares at me. "Anything else?" I shake my head. I'm completely drawn to my eye, the color change is intriguing. "You've done well, Lexi. Put your gloves back on and enjoy the rest of the evening." He stands and holds his hand to me.

"Can we leave? I don't want to socialize with anyone, and I did what you asked. Please?"

"No, we have to have dinner. I don't want to arouse any suspicions. Especially about you."

"Ugh, fine," I complain.

Jude stands and leads me out of the powder room toward a grand dining room. There's several round tables set, all beautifully decorated with an abundance of fresh, colorful flowers. The lights are dim, though it's still bright enough to see the extravagance, as if someone is showing off all their money. My eyes take in everything, from the two huge chandeliers hanging overhead, to the big band set up on stage. "Are you appreciating all of this?" Jude asks before taking my seat out so I can sit.

"It's over the top if you ask me. These things don't impress me, what would impress me is if drugs and whatever else has bought this . . ." I sweep my hand across the room indicating the sheer opulence, " . . . wasn't so easily accessible to ruin people's lives."

Jude scoffs and places his elbows on the table, steepling them together. "You never cease to surprise me, Lexi."

"Why?" I retort with a bark to my tone. He's being condescending toward me, and I'm not about to let him think I'm a dumb schoolkid.

"Because the war on drugs is futile. Someone is always trying to make a quick dollar, and what better way to do so than drugs?" he challenges me.

I think long and hard about his response. He's right about one thing, trying to stamp out drugs would be like trying to saving a sinking ship armed with only a bucket. Therefore, I speak on the terms he'd understand. "What about prostitution?"

His brows fly up in surprise. He takes a deep breath, runs one of his hands over his face then lets out a small snicker. "What about prostitution?"

"It's the oldest profession in the world. Can't you do away with drugs and run brothels?"

"You're suggesting I force women into the sex industry?"

Whoa! "Back up a second, buddy. I said nothing about forcing anyone." He sits back in his seat and crosses his arms in front of his chest, clearly amused at me. "Wipe that stupid smirk off your face." He struggles, but he lowers the corners of his lips. However, the smile is now in his eyes. "What I'm saying, is offer a safe place to work, good money, good clientele, have certain standards for the women and for the clients, and make money that way."

People are still filtering in and filling the tables. The women are staring at Jude and quickly glancing over to me, basically ignoring me while trying to get Jude's attention. His attentiveness doesn't falter, and other than a few head nods and shaking of hands, he essentially shuts them out.

"Interesting," he mumbles while looking around the room. "You're quite progressive in your way of thinking. Most people would say prostitution is as harmful as drugs or firearms. But you're suggesting an alternative to drugs and guns. But is prostitution the answer? Unfortunately, this world isn't pleasant. It isn't glittery rainbows and unicorns. It isn't nice. The moment I step down, or die, they'll be a hundred-people waiting to fight it out for my position."

This of course raises more questions. "Then why haven't you been killed off already? If it's as cutthroat as you're making it out to be, then you should've been . . . what's the technical term you'd use? Bumped off?"

A small plate is placed in front of me, I look down at the incredibly teeny tiny appetizer.

"You amuse me, Lexi. The only way for me to die is if one of my own people kill me, or I die of old age. I'm well protected. *Very* well protected." He inhales the tiny portion of food, and looks at mine. "You going to eat that?" He pointedly looks down at my small plate.

"Yes, I'm going to eat it. Whatever it is. Sheesh." I pick up my fork.

In less than three bites, my plate is clean. Not a crumb is left on it. "You liked it?"

"It's food. Can we go back to why we're even here?"

"To raise money for a halfway house."

"Come on, seriously? You can't see the humor in that?"

"It's a tax write-off for me."

Picking up the water glass, my hand stills and I laugh. "You pay taxes? Like, for real? You don't strike me as a man who'd declare your income or how you earned it."

An unusual sound captures my attention and I turn to look. It's like something's being dragged along at even intervals. As I investigate the rhythmic clamor, my eyes go directly to the source. A man limping, almost dragging his leg behind him. "That's him," I whisper to Jude.

"Who?" He leans over to look at the direction my head is turned.

"Him," I whisper, turning back when Limpy's gaze reaches mine. "The guy who was talking to Alfred."

"Ahhh," Jude announces slowly. "I knew Alfred was going to cause me problems, but Mario . . . I'm surprised."

"Mario is Limpy?"

"Limpy?" Jude questions me.

I smack his leg lightly and laugh to myself. "I gave him a name because I didn't know what his was. I shouldn't judge, but that's what stuck out for me."

Jude places his hand on my arm, and squeezes. My stupid heart decides right at this moment to spike in beats causing my stupid face to smile at his stupid touch. *Stupid me.*

Ugh.

"You really do amuse me."

One plate is taken away and another is placed in front of me.

This one has more food than the appetizer. Jude and I quietly eat but the entire time his eyes are on me or on Alfred who's sitting two tables away and has his back to us. Limpy is at another table altogether and nowhere near Alfred. "Did you know they knew each other?" I ask following his line of sight.

"This business is large, but everyone knows everyone else. For instance," he stops talking and grabs a waiter who's walking past with champagne. "Who am I?" he asks the young male waiter.

The waiter's ears quickly turn pink, and he looks down at his feet. "You're Mr. Caley, Sir." Jude flicks his wrist at the waiter, who turns and gets away from us as quickly as possible.

"Some of us don't need introductions, and for some of us, our reputation is known quite widely."

"You get off on people being scared of you."

"I must admit, it has its advantages," he adds cockily.

"Because people are frightened. So, it's a power thing for you?" I know at any moment he can snap at me, maybe even hit me, but if I'm stuck in his world at least I can try to understand him.

"People's basic nature is to control others, to tell them what to do, boss them around. For me, yes, it's a power thing. I like walking into a room and watching people either quiver with fear, or be aroused and want to fuck me. I enjoy watching people and their reactions, and I love it even more when they're begging for their lives in front of me. There's a look a person gets when they're about to die, it's not in their face, or even the tension in their body. It's in their eyes. Seconds before they die, they realize everything they've done that has caused that one particular moment to happen."

Jude's words are quite horrifying to me, and I can't help but think how much of an animal he is. His words *are* disturbing, but he says them with so much conviction and pride. He's opening a part of himself to me that I doubt many people get to see, and I have no idea why he's sharing so much with me. I know I ask questions, but this seems so personal to him, intimate . . . *passionate.*

There's a fire in his eyes, a spark which nearly crosses over into obsession, and maybe that's what this is for him. I sincerely doubt Jude will ever leave this lifestyle, I can see how in love with it he is.

"You're a frightening man, Jude." My words have interrupted his nostalgic recount of how he feels being the man he is.

"But never to you."

"Oh no, you scare the shit out of me too. I'm waiting for the day you snap and kill me, or beat me."

He pulls his head back; his face stamped with concern and worry. "Because I've hurt you while you've been with me?"

"Been with you? You make it seem like I want to be here."

"Well . . ." he begins saying but I hold my hand up to halt whatever he's going to say.

"I know the conditions, and I'm slowly learning to accept them, but it still doesn't mean I *want* to be here."

Jude sighs, and then smiles. He stands abruptly and offers me his hand. "Dance?" he asks. I look around the room and notice not one person is dancing to the soft background music being played by the ten-piece orchestra.

"No one's dancing." I straighten my back and realize a few people are turning their heads toward Jude. "And, people are staring."

"You worry too much about what everyone else is thinking. Dance with me." He thrusts his hand closer.

Defiantly I jut my chin out and say, "I don't know how to." Ha! He can look like a fool at my resistance.

Jude tilts his head to the side and smirks at me. "Says the girl whose parents gave dance lessons to from the age of eight until fifteen."

My own grin quickly is wiped away and replaced with my mouth falling open. "Figures." I stand and Jude pushes my chair in once I've stepped to the side. "I forgot you were a stalker." I lay my gloved hand in his and he leads us over to the isolated dance floor. The entire room is quiet as all eyes are glued to us. "Great, they're all staring."

"Why wouldn't they? You look breathtaking, and they all want to know who you are."

He wraps his left hand around my waist, drawing me in close to him, and tightens his right hand around mine. He's taller than me, and his broad shoulders are nothing but intimidating. "I've never been the type who loves being the center of attention, so I'm feeling quite uncomfortable right now."

"Because I'm holding you tightly or because everyone is staring?"

Cocky asswipe. "Both," I whisper and look around the room. "Most the people in here are staring at us, and I'm not liking it." My heartbeat is steadily increasing, and my palms sweat. Thank goodness, I'm wearing gloves—even though they're the most disgusting gloves ever made.

"Don't worry about them, just keep looking at me." He moves his hand from my waist, and gently tilts my head to gaze up at him.

His moves may work on others, but I'm not 'others.' "You're not going to get laid, Jude. I don't find you attractive at all." It's a lie, 'cause I think he's hot. It's the whole 'killer' and 'let's kidnap Lexi' thing turning me off.

"Oh, I'm going to get laid, Lexi." He smiles at me cheekily. "It just won't be you."

My heart breaks a tiny amount, but I pull my shoulders back and smile at Jude. "Can we go now, please?" I ask again.

"We still need to finish the rest of our meal."

Anger snaps through me and I step back, breaking the tight hold Jude has on me. "I'm going to walk out in five seconds, Jude. I no longer want to be here."

He lets go of my waist, and holds my hand. "Then let's go home."

He's taking such large steps out of the ballroom that I'm practically running to keep up with him. He's tugging on my hand, dragging me behind. As soon as we're outside, the car we came in pulls around to the front. Jude opens the door and almost forcefully pushes me in. "Jude," I try and say, but his cold features and angry eyes tell me all I need to know.

He leans over, pours a drink, and lifts the glass to his lips. Essentially, he's telling me he no longer wants to discuss anything with me. *Point taken.*

But here's the thing, he's taken me out of my home and is forcing me to stay with him and perform like a damn circus monkey for *him.*

My anger is bubbling over, my leg starts to jump as I get madder with every mile traveled. He's an asswipe. A self-centered, arrogant, asshole. It seems like the drive back is taking forever. The more he ignores me, the angrier I get.

When the car pulls up outside his stupid house, I get out and slam the door with so much fury. "You're such an asshole," I finally yell at Jude. I walk around to the side he's at, and poke him in the chest. "You kidnapped me, you brought me here, and you're forcing me to work for you. And now, you're being a total douche bag, creeper, asshole, prick!" I poke my finger into his chest again, then turn and walk toward the house.

I hear him gurgle with laughter from behind me, but can feel him right there, close to me. The door opens and one of his stupid security guards is standing at the door. "Boss," he says as I barge past him and head toward my room.

"Lexi!" Jude calls, but I ignore him and make my way up the grand staircase. "Lexi!" he says again from behind me. Still ignoring him, I stomp in the direction of my room. "Alexa!"

I freeze with the sound of his voice. He's not yelling, there's more desperation than anger. It's almost like his tone is laced with urgency. "No! No, Jude just no." I come to stand face to face with him. "You do *not* get to call the shots here, buddy. You do not bring me into this lifestyle and make me part of it, then ignore me in the fucking car. You have no right to do the shit you're doing. You have no right to say what you're saying, and you have no right to be . . ." I wave my hand over him from head to toe. " . . . to be like that!"

He steps closer, my heartbeat increases. God, why does he have to look so good? Why does he have to affect me like this? I hate myself for finding him attractive.

"Be like what?" he asks. A sly smirk tugs on his lips.

"You're an ass, Jude." I shake my head at him and turn to walk away.

I get no more than two steps before I feel his hand on my upper arm, stopping me from going anywhere. He swings me around, causing my body to fling into his. He looks down at me, and for a split-second I lose my concentration and the anger that was building inside of me.

"You know, it's unhealthy to go to sleep angry." He lifts his hand to gently skim it down the side of my face. He almost touches my flamed skin, when he pulls back.

"That's only if we were in a relationship, and what we have is *not* a relationship." I step back, slowing my uneven heartbeat, and calming my weak knees.

I'm so angry at myself. He shows me his nice side and suddenly I like him. He dresses-up and acts like a gentleman, and I fall for it.

"Lexi," he calls again from behind me as I walk away.

I ignore him, and go straight to my jail. Slamming the door, I stand and look around the room. This is definitely my holding cell. It might be pretty, it might look normal, but there's nothing normal about it. Tears prickle my eyes as an overwhelming sense of sadness hits me in the chest.

I crumple against the door, sliding down until my butt hits the floor. I want to go home and hug my parents. I want to get out of here. My hot tears are falling fast, as my body shivers from my hurting heart.

"I want to go home, Jude!" I yell as I grasp my head and cry even more. "Let me go home." The tears won't stop. I can't control them, they keep falling.

Sobbing wildly, I stand from the floor and head into the bathroom. Looking at my reflection in the mirror, I gasp at how terrible I look. My skin is blotchy, my eyes are red and the mascara is lining my spotted skin.

"This is bullshit," I say as I wipe my face and try to regain a grip on myself. The huge lump sitting at the base of my throat eases as my crying stops. Staring into the mirror, I blink away the tears and take several deep breaths. "You can do this."

I slide the dress off my body and take the stupid, ugly gloves off. Walking out to my room, I look around at what's in here. I rock the bedside table, and notice, with a bit of effort, I can move it. Dragging it over to where the camera is; I grab one of the gloves, and stand on top of the table. As I reach up on my tiptoes, I manage to slide the glove over the camera. Jumping off, I push the table back over to beside the bed.

The white chest of drawers beside the window has nothing in it considering all the clothes are in the walk-in wardrobe. I push it in front of the door. If he's going to keep me here, I refuse to let him, or any other bastard waltz in here whenever they want.

This is my space, and I control who comes in, not that sick bastard who thinks he can do what he wants with me. This is my domain, and not his.

Flopping on the bed proudly, the onset of sadness takes over again. This is so hard. I'm only seventeen, what am I supposed to do? I can't live here forever, I'll go crazy.

The tears take over again, and I break down, hugging the second pillow on the bed. I want my Dad to give me a kiss on the cheek and to tell me everything's going to be okay. When I used to get sick, Dad would stay with me all night to make sure I didn't get worse. He'd tie my hair back, and apply a wet washcloth to my forehead. He's always been my Superman, the best man in the entire world.

I miss Dad so much. All I want to do is hug him, and hug Mom. Mom may have worked a lot, but I know she loves me more than her life. I know that me 'missing' would be tearing them apart.

Crying into the pillow, my sobs finally ease, and my mind begins to settle and accept my life as it is.

Perhaps, it's my curse.

CHAPTER 15

OPENING MY EYES to the sun streaming into the room, I feel like a train has hit me. My body is sore and my eyes feel puffy.

Letting out a deep breath, I cuddle into the pillow further. Looking out the window, I try to find the strength to drag myself out of bed. I want to stay in here forever, but my bladder isn't happy with me refusing to get up.

Sitting up in bed, I sigh again.

"Good morning," Jude says from behind me.

I yelp in fright. Turning to face him, I quickly look at the overturned chest of drawers. How did I not hear that? "What are you doing here?" I snap at him. "Don't you get it, Jude, I wanted privacy. And this proves how you're incapable of giving it to me." I point to the overturned drawers while walking past him to the bathroom. "By the way, I'm going to the toilet, do you want to watch that too?" Slamming the door shut gives me a small amount of satisfaction.

Taking my time in the bathroom, I'm hoping he'll be gone, but knowing how cocky and smug he is guarantees he'll still be in my bedroom.

Opening the door, I strut out and find him sitting on the bed. "What do you want?" I bark toward him.

"I'm here because we're having breakfast together."

"Why?" I walk past him into the wardrobe and look at the

array of clothes. Choosing a pair of jeans and a t-shirt, I head back into the bedroom. Throwing my clothes on the bed, next to Jude, I stand and stare at him. "You gonna watch as I get dressed?"

He smirks at me, crosses his legs, and nods his head. *Arrogant ass.*

"Fine." I put a show on for him. I slept in my bra and undies last night, so it's not like he can't see my body, but I flirt it right up. He wants to be a bastard, then I'll teach him.

Heading into the closet, I grab the sexiest bra and cutest pair of undies I can find. A black number with loads of lace, but I still make sure they cover everything.

Leaving the closest, I stand in front of Jude and smile. "Well, this should be fun," he says in his overconfident but sexy voice.

"It will be," I reply, equally as assured and smug. Keeping my eyes on his, I reach back and flick open the bra clasps. The sides fling out and I let my hands drop to my side. Jude's eyes go directly to my breasts. He fidgets slightly, and I smile. The bra straps fall down my arms, and Jude straightens his back, ready to see me exposed. "Do you like what you see?"

He doesn't need to respond; his reaction is enough for me to know the answer.

"Um," he clears his throat. "It's adequate," he arrogantly mutters. But the crack in his voice screams what he's really thinking. He's turned on. And this gives me the power — even if it's only for a minute, *I'm* in command.

Lifting my hand, I slowly help the strap further down my arm. The top of my breast is nearly exposed, though my nipple is still hidden.

Jude swallows and the pompous grin on his face, drops.

I push the strap down further, Jude sits up straighter and moves forward. As I push the strap down, the cup begins to peel back, revealing my breast. Jude sits more forward. Before he has a chance to look at my boob, I cover it with my hand.

"Oh God," he whispers, his eyes devouring me.

With my free hand, I grab the bra, and swing it from my little finger. "You sure I'm only 'adequate'?" I ask putting on a cutesy voice.

"You're really quite . . ." He doesn't say anything else. The muscles in his legs jump.

Turning so my back is to him, in quick as lightning speed, I slip off the bra I slept in, and change to the clean one. I hear Jude grumble, and him shifting on the bed. I turn to look at him from over my shoulder and do the whole blink like I'm flirting thing. "Oh, you're still here," I say, catching him staring at my butt.

"I am . . ." He extends his neck and adjusts his shirt collar. "I'm waiting for you to get ready so I can take you to breakfast."

"And where exactly are we going?"

He's still staring at my butt.

He doesn't say anything.

"I must be talking to myself," I say as I turn and stand in front of him in my bra and undies.

He swallows hard, again. His eyes are consuming every inch of exposed skin. The tension in the room changes again, and it's obvious how my presence is *affecting* him. "Um . . ." He abruptly stands and turns so I can't see his face, and *other* parts. "Be ready in two minutes and meet me at the bottom of the stairs." *Two minutes, really is that all it's going to take?* His steps are long and rapid. He's trying to get out of here as quickly as possible but he stops by the door. Without turning his head to look at me, he says with his deep drawl, "And by the way, Lexi, I am not gay."

The door slams shut and I'm left perplexed by his response.

It takes me a full minute to realize what he means by it. When I saw the evening gown, I said he must be gay because gay men have good fashion sense. Obviously, he heard me. Confirms exactly what I think of him, he's a pervert who listens and watches me.

Chuckling, I take the rest of the clothes into the bathroom and get changed there.

"You look beautiful," he says as I make my way down the stairs.

"Thank you," I reply as kindly as I can. He's trying not to be the kidnapper, the threat he really is. I suppose I should be thankful he's not hurting me. Or worse, forcing me into being a sex slave. "Where are you taking me?"

"Out for breakfast."

"So you've said," I sarcastically respond. "A name would be good."

Jude looks at me, frustration flashing across his face. "Does it matter, Lexi? Does the name of where I'm taking you actually make a difference?"

I shrug and look down at my feet. "S'pose not."

"Then just enjoy it." He steps toward the front door, and the guy dressed in all black, stands to the side as he opens the door for us. The black limousine is waiting for us.

Taking a moment, I inhale a deep breath, closing my eyes and tilting my head up toward the sky. "It smells like rain," I whisper. "I love the smell of rain on freshly cut grass. It's exactly what I can smell." The scent is intoxicating. It reminds me of summer rains and Dad mowing the lawn while Mom and I sit on the back deck watching him. It reminds me of cold watermelon, and homemade lemonade. It reminds me of home.

A place I'll never go to again.

The sadness clouds every beautiful memory. My body reacts with instant stiffness in my neck and tears welling in my eyes.

"Lexi, are you okay?' he asks, stepping closer to me.

"In all the things you bought me, did you buy me sunglasses?" I keep my head down, because I don't want him to see that he has the power to make me this sad.

"I didn't."

"Buy me some today," I say assertively. I quickly wipe at my eyes, straighten my back, and hold my chin up.

He will *not* break me.

"Of course," he replies. His voice is filled with worry.

"I wasn't asking." Screw him. I need my parents, I don't need him.

The driver chuckles and Jude snaps his head to the side to glare at him. Jude's jaw clenches shut, his square jawline grinds together. "Get in the car, Lexi." I slide in and he slams the door shut so hard, it makes the car shake.

The sadness I was holding is now replaced by fear. He walks around to the driver, grabs him by the scruff of the neck and slams his head down on the car, making the car vibrate all over again.

"Shit!" I squeak with horror and clap my hand to my mouth. My widened eyes can't look away at what's happening. Jude lifts the guy by knotting his fist into his hair; he slams the guy's face down on the car again and again and *again*.

"Jude!" I yell. He stops slamming the guy's head, and looks through the window at me.

My entire body is quivering with dread and horror. Jude's features soften when he sees my petrified reaction. Straightening, the guy slides down the car, just like in the movies, and Jude steps back from him. He adjusts his tailored jacket and rolls his shoulders, all while keeping his eyes on me. Turning his head, he spits on the ground. His breathing is labored. Jude looks to the door, breaking eye contact with me for a split second as he gives directions to whoever he's talking with.

He comes to the back of the car, opens the door and slides in. "My apologies you had to see that," he says casually.

I scoot over as far away from him and close to the opposite door as possible. I'm so close, I'm almost hugging it.

"You hurt him," I manage to whisper shocked and fearfully.

"Yes," he responds with authority.

"Because of me. It wasn't his fault, Jude, it was mine. You shouldn't have . . ." I don't say anymore except point toward the front of the car.

"It has nothing to do with you." He wipes his hands down the front of his designer pants and leans over to the bottle of amber liquid, pouring himself a drink.

With shaking hands, I snatch it and throw it down my throat, not waiting for him to offer or say anything. When I finish, I hand him the glass. "It's because I was being a smart ass toward you that he laughed."

"He had it coming."

He pours another drink and offers it to me, but the burn in my throat from the first drink is a memento that drinking and I don't mix. I shake my head and look out the window. I hear the drivers' door slam shut and I look forward, noticing the driver isn't the guy with the bashed-in face. "What um . . . is the guy . . ." I swallow back the tears and try to keep it together. "Is he going to be okay?"

I can barely keep my eyes on Jude, he's shown me a side of him that's making my skin crawl with fear. He shrugs and knocks the drink back in one movement. "Whatever happens to him is on him, not you."

I'm fighting all these emotions building inside me. I miss my parents, I want to leave and now I got a guy's head bashed in because I've been fighting Jude and being smart to him.

"This isn't right, Jude, none of this is normal." I burst into tears, crying into my hands. "It's too much for me to handle."

"Hey," he says putting his arm around me, dragging me toward him, but making sure he's not touching my bare skin.

"Please, don't," I beg. "My head's a mess. All of this is a one huge pile of shit."

"You know where to go," Jude says to the driver. He raises the privacy screen while my crying continues. He hugs me closer, and as much as I hate the fact he's the one to console me, I'm also drawing on his warmth. *Warmth of a monster.*

"Jude, I'm trying my best to not screw everything up for my parents and Dallas. But you can't do things like that and not expect me to react." I point backward toward the house. "It puts a lot of responsibility on me. I'm only just seventeen and I'm wrestling with this thing I have no idea how to control. Please, I can't do this." I cry into his chest. He hugs me tighter, and strokes my hair down my back.

"You can." He kisses my head.

"I hate you so much."

"I want to believe you, but I don't." He kisses me again.

My tears won't stop, and I wish he'd let me go. But at this point, I know he'll never let me leave. The only way I'll be able to go anywhere, is in a body bag.

Crying into his chest, I close my eyes tightly and wish I never got this stupid gift, the bane of my existence.

I'm not sure how long we're in the car, but when it finally stops I pull away from Jude and look out the window. We've stopped on the side of the busiest street in the city. The driver gets out and comes to open my door. "Ma'am," he says holding his hand out for me.

"Don't touch her," Jude barks from beside me.

Quietly grumbling, I'm getting sick of the way Jude talks to his people. But I pull it back the moment I realize the driver notices my reaction. I don't want to be responsible for anyone else getting hurt.

I wait on the footpath for Jude. He comes to stand beside me, sliding gloves on his hands. He reaches down and grabs my hand in his. "This way," he says as we enter the lobby of a prestigious hotel.

There's a doorman waiting for us, dressed in a top hat and light gray suit. "Sir, Ma'am," he says as we enter. I give him a warm smile, then cast down my eyes, knowing they're puffy and red.

"What are we doing here?" I ask.

"I told you, breakfast." He leads me over to the elevators, presses the up arrow and waits. "What happened with the driver, had nothing to do with you," he says again.

"I'm getting a headache; can we not talk about it? I'm going to try and erase it from my brain." My head is thumping, it feels like my brain has swollen so much my head is going to explode.

"I hope you're hungry." He squeezes my hand, turns, and smiles down at me.

I'm in no mood for anything, but I have to make sure I don't get someone else hurt, or killed. "Sure thing," I say and muster the weakest smile I can offer.

"After breakfast we'll get you sunglasses. Do you want anything else? Need it?"

Ugh, what a stupid question. Yes, I need to go home. "No," I say. "Actually, I'm due for my period, and I need female products." I look up at Jude, and notice his cheeks pink. "Seriously?"

"What?"

"You can hurt a man with your bare hands, but the moment I mention periods, you go red."

He shudders and looks away. The elevator dings and the door opens to a big empty foyer. Awaiting us on the floor is one of Jude's body guards. This guy has to be the biggest guy I've ever seen. He's three times the size of Jude, and has shoulders so wide I swear he can barely fit through the elevator doors. Okay, it's an over exaggeration. He's not that big, but man, he's intimidating. He looks like he can stop a bullet with his hands, or eat a medium-sized animal in one sitting.

"It's not exactly something I've ever had to worry about. Having you around is new to me too."

Having me around? *You mean kidnapping me?* "We all have to adjust to the situation." I let out a sigh. The doors open to another elevator beside the one we got out of, and another big guy barrels out. "Why don't you have one guy with you? They're always changing." I eye his bodyguards.

"I only trust one person. I keep rotating everyone else so people aren't aware of everything happening in my life."

"Clear, boss," one of the bodyguards says.

He only trusts one person, I wonder who it is. Have we met yet?

We walk a few steps into a restaurant and we're immediately lead to the back, where a private room has been set up. "Wow," I gasp in awe as I head to the huge floor to ceiling windows. "Look at these views!" I lean my hand against the window and look out at the tops of the buildings. It's breathtakingly beautiful. I've never seen the city from such heights.

"I'm okay," Jude says from somewhere behind me.

Turning, I find him sitting in one of two plush chairs watching me. "Come have a look."

"I'm fine where I am."

I look behind him to find the big guy standing guard over the door. I want to call him on it, being afraid of heights, but if the guy laughs, I'm afraid what may happen to him. Instead I sigh and smile. "Suit yourself," I reply and turn to keep gazing over the city. "It's so clear. I can see people swimming in the rooftop pool over there." I point toward the pool, but Jude is too far to see.

"Do you enjoy the city?" Turning back to Jude, I lean against the window pane. Because we're so high up, the window is incredibly cool to touch, the cold saturating my skin. Before I answer Jude's question, he jumps out if his seat and moves in my direction. "Can you step away from there, please?" He holds his hand out for to me to take. The bodyguard moves closer to me too.

"Why? I'm safe here."

"It'll make me feel better if you'd just come closer to me." He motions with his hand to move away from the glass.

I look at the bodyguard, then back to Jude. Images of the ex-driver flood my brain. It's best I do as Jude wants, because any smart ass remark from me has the potential for getting more people hurt. *This is so frustrating.*

"Okay." I leave the coolness of the window, and head over to the table set with crystal and china. Sitting in the chair opposite

Jude I glance down to expensive plates in front of us.

"What would you like to drink?" Jude offers.

Seconds later a male waiter arrives with a cart filled with juices, water, and silver pots. "Coffee, juice, or perhaps I can get something else for you? Hot chocolate? Tea? Something alcoholic?" The young waiter looks to Jude, me then back to Jude.

"Lexi?" Jude encourages.

"Orange juice, thanks."

"Coffee, black," Jude says in a deadpan voice. *Just like his soul.*

The guy gets our drinks ready, then wheels the cart out. "Why are we here on our own?"

"Because I'm not a fan of people. They always let me down, and I'm not partial to the looks and stares."

"You being self-conscious is the last thing I'd ever expect you to say."

"Do I strike you as self-conscious? I just don't like people in general."

Drawing my brows together, I can't help but think how he's been with me. Although this situation is wrong, he hasn't mistreated me or man-handled me. But being out in public, also makes me think of another question. "Jude, what if someone recognizes me?"

"What do you mean?" He sips his coffee.

"Are you serious? You've taken me. My Mom is a judge, an *influential* judge. I doubt she'd be sitting around doing nothing. I'm positive she would have pulled every favor she could in order to find me. And with facial recognition software so readily available, and me out in public, who knows how many people have already recognized me and have alerted authorities."

"No one will alert police," he casually replies like I've said nothing alarming.

"And you know this for sure?"

The waiter wheels in another cart and stops beside the table.

He places no less than eight dome-covered plates on the table, then leaves without saying a word.

Jude uncovers all the plates; each being revealed more delicious than the one before. Eggs, bacon, pancakes, waffles, oatmeal, muffins, crepes, and French toast. "Yum, but is there any fruit?" I ask.

"Is that what you want? Some fruit?"

"Your chef is feeding me well, but yeah, I need some fruit."

Jude turns his head to look at the bodyguard, and flicks his wrist at him. He leaves, closing the door behind him. "He'll get you fruit."

"Thank you." I grab a blueberry muffin and nibble on it. My stomach is still rolling from the violent image of this morning. "Jude, I'm scared," I honestly admit.

"Of me?" I think for a minute, then nod my head. "I don't want you to be scared of me, Lexi. Ever."

"But I am. By your own admission, you said you only trust one person and don't want anyone knowing the full extent of your business. And there's going to be a time, when I'll know. Regardless of how I know, through a vision, or by being witness to it." I look off to the side and sigh. "I'm going to know. Which means, my life expectancy has dramatically decreased."

He lets out a roar of a laugh and reaches over to the French toast. He takes the entire plate, pours maple syrup over it, and starts to inhale them. "You have nothing to worry about with me."

"You say this like you know for sure. Like you said about no one recognizing me and calling the police. How do you know, Jude?" My tone increases as frustration overtakes.

"Because I have the police in my pocket."

Bad trumps good.

"Of course, you do." A small part of me knew he's capable of something so grand. Another question comes to mind. "Is my Mom part of the people in your pocket?" Tears sting my eyes. I don't want to know if she is. I'm begging and praying he says no.

He shakes his head. "She can't be bought. A lot of people have tried. She's straight."

Relief overtakes me. As much as I know my Mom is a good person, since I've been with Jude, I've seen a different side to life. A side I never want to be part of, but unfortunately I am.

The bodyguard enters the room, and brings over two large plates with an array of fruit. "They'll bring more, boss," he says with his deep, gravelly voice. This guy has the look of the devil in his eyes. He can hurt someone, and not care.

"I don't need any more." I eye the giant selection on the plate.

"They'll be in with more in a minute, boss."

I must be invisible. That's what it is.

"We don't need any more," Jude replies to the big guy and he leaves the room, closing the door again.

I pick at my food, while my thoughts are consumed by my parents. I'm thankful they're not in Jude's pocket. They're good people. I always knew they were, but Jude confirming it eases my heart.

CHAPTER 16

"**W**HERE ARE WE going now?" I ask as the car pulls up in front of a tall building with no name on it.

"You need sunglasses. We're getting you sunglasses."

"And pads and tampons." Jude shudders again, and I can't help but laugh at his reaction. "I'm sure you've had plenty of female company in your life, Jude." I mean, he's tall, he has the sexiest, most compelling eyes, not to mention his jawline. *Snap out of it, Lexi.* "You can't tell me you've never held onto a girl long enough for a cycle of her periods."

"First, you're way too open in talking about . . ." He makes a circular motion toward my stomach and his face turns up in a grimace. "And second, I'm not a 'let's have a relationship' kinda guy."

"Ewww. Imagine the diseases you could have," I automatically respond to his comment and return his circling motion toward his crotch region. "And second, my parents have brought me up to be open and honest with everything."

He shakes his head; his lips turn down, and he's clearly revolted by the whole 'period' thing. "You can't go talking about things like periods."

"Why not? It's part of a female's life. You had to know this would come up at some point considering you . . . you know . . . kidnapped me!"

"It's not how I imagined it to be."

"Sorry, buddy, you've got to deal. Just like I have to adjust to living with a sociopath who thinks it's okay to beat people up, you have to deal with living with a female who will bleed once a month until the day I die."

"Don't you go through menopause? You'll stop bleeding then."

"Jude, really? Look at this lifestyle you lead. Do you honestly expect to live long enough to see me reach menopause?"

Jude looks at me, his face scrunched in question. He looks back out to the building and runs his hand through his hair, frustrated. "Look, do you want these damn glasses or not? I'm not sitting here arguing with you about when my life will end."

"Fine," I say, opening the door without taking any notice of oncoming traffic. Jude quickly exits the car, completely amused. "What are we doing here anyway?"

"How did you get through life? I swear you don't listen. Sunglasses." When I get to the pavement I notice Jude putting on gloves, *again*. "Come on, I don't have all day." He holds his hand out to me. I don't want to take it, but I do because I don't want a repeat performance of the driver from this morning.

We enter an incredibly plain building and he leads me past the concierge who gives him a small nod and passes him an electronic keycard. Jude keeps walking at his fast pace, and I'm nearly running to keep up with him. "What's the hurry?" I say almost breathless.

"Keep up," he playfully barks as he looks over his shoulder to me.

We head down a long, isolated corridor, and suddenly my heart stops beating. "Wait up!" I halt my movements.

"What?"

"I've seen enough criminal shows to know you're about to bump me off, right?"

"What is it with you and death?"

"Well, look around. The corridors are isolated. You're wearing gloves, which normally would scare the shit out of me, but combined with being in such a rush, I think you're taking me somewhere to kill me." Completely illogical, yes, I know.

"Of course, which is why I fed you first, so you die with a full stomach."

"Where you're taking me, is it a room lined with plastic sheets?"

"I swear to God," he mumbles, continuing forward.

"If there's plastic sheets, can you at least pre-warn me? No, wait. Don't warn me."

"Stop talking."

"No! Warn me. No . . . don't. Shit, Jude. Are you going to kill me or not?"

"No, but I'm going to tape your mouth if you don't shut up."

"So, no killing then?"

He swipes the card at the door, and we leave the building and enter the back of another using the same swipe key. "No killing."

"But you're taking me around the world. I swear you're going to kill me."

He chuckles loudly and tugs on my hand as we go down yet another, cold and sterile corridor. "For the love of God, just shut up."

He stops at another door, swipes his card, and holds it open for me. We're in a spotlessly clean room, and instantly my body shivers with excitement that he's not going to hack me into a million pieces and feed me to the fish.

The small room has floor to ceiling shelves, and is packed tight with boxes stacked on top of one another. "Just checking." I peer down at the floor, and stomp my feet. "Nope, no plastic. I live to talk another day."

"Lexi, you're killing me." Jude laughs.

"Is this our stop?"

"It is. Now we wait." He looks at his gold watch, then lifts his head toward the door. As if he's psychic, the door opens and a really cute, and very bouncy brunette enters. "Stevie," he says and moves forward to kiss her on the cheek.

This Stevie chick turns her head and lands a kiss on Jude's mouth. She laces her fingers into his hair and pulls him down to her. Her eyes are open, and she's looking straight at me. Warning me, showing me exactly the hold she has over him.

He pulls away and I can't help but glare at her. She's being a bitch, but who am I to give a crap who he kisses and who he doesn't? She can have him.

But the knot in my stomach is telling me something else.

"Who's this, Jude baby?"

I cringe the moment I hear her high-pitched voice. Like nails dragging down a chalk board. *Gross.*

"This is Alexa. She's a very good friend of mine."

Stevie drapes herself around Jude, her eyes travel up and down my body checking me out. We're just missing the chewing of gum to make her super cliché.

I put my bitch face on, and hold my hand out to hers. "Alexa. Pleased to meet you."

She hesitantly grabs my hand and I flash Jude a look. One that tells him I'm about to find out every one of her dirty little secrets.

I'm in her bedroom. She's standing in front of her full-length mirror, fixing her boobs while she's puckering her lips. She looks like a duck's butt when she crumples her mouth like that. She grabs her phone, puckers again, pushes her chest out and takes a selfie then sends it to someone. She's pleased with herself, because she smiles and lifts her brows seductively. *Like anyone can see her.*

I gaze around the room, and try to move toward her bedside table. I've only been able to move in my first vision, and I've not been able to do it again. I look down at my feet, and will them to move. They feel like lead, heavy as boulders. But with sheer determination I manage to move, and what feels like forever later, I'm standing by her bedside where she's placed her phone.

Leaning down, I swipe at her screen, but my hand goes

through the phone. "Damn it," I grumble as I try to unlock it to see whom she's sent the selfie to.

"Hello?" Stevie says as she turns in her room to face me.

My heart skips a beat, and I hold my breath. *She can hear me?* No one has ever heard me before.

"Hello? Is someone there?" she calls again, stepping closer toward me.

"Stevie, I've been calling you for ten minutes." An older woman bursts through her door, she's holding a baby on her hip. "You need to come feed this baby." Her eyes travel Stevie's body before she shakes her head. "You're not going out looking like that." With her free hand, the woman shakes her finger at Stevie.

"Mom, I found out Jude will be at the club tonight."

Suddenly I feel sick to my stomach. Is that little baby Jude's?

"So what if he's at the club?" her mother barks at Stevie.

"I'm gonna tell him the baby's his," Stevie shrieks at her mom. "Can't you feed her?"

My heart drops into the pit of my stomach and I feel my breakfast lunge toward making a grand exit.

"You think a man like Jude Caley won't do a paternity test? Then what will you do when he finds out it's not his? How will you handle that?" The mom tries to give Stevie the baby, but Stevie goes back to touching up her lipstick. "And what about Brenden? He won't like you chasing another man."

"Momma, you worry too much. I'm only going after Jude because he has money. And once he accepts Bella as his, he'll do everything to keep Bella and me happy. Don't worry, he'll be eating out of the palm of my hand." She twirls around as if she's something special.

"Stevie, this is ri . . ."

And I'm back in the store room, Jude's watching me, and Stevie turns her back.

My throat is parched, and my knees wobble from a sudden onset of weakness. "I need to sit," I whisper hoarsely as my legs nearly give. I sway and Jude catches me before I fall.

"Are you okay?" he asks kneeling in front of me.

Stevie turns to look at me, snarling and rolling her eyes. "She's fine," she snaps.

"I'd like some water, please?" I smile at her, making her sneer even more.

"Get her some water, Stevie," Jude growls at her.

If looks could kill, I'd be dead a thousand times over from the intense glare Stevie is aiming at me. Thankfully, she leaves, but not before lifting her top lip at me, almost baring her teeth. *Freak.*

"Are you okay? What happened?" Jude asks.

"I moved."

Standing from the kneeling position, he steps backward a step. "What do you mean?"

"I've only ever been able to move in the very first vision I had, and the rest since then feel like my feet are glued. But I managed to move. I wanted to see who she texted that ridiculous selfie to."

"Here's your water, princess," Stevie throws a bottle of water at me, but Jude catches it before it hits me. And let me tell you, she was throwing it *at* me to make sure it caused a bruise.

I don't see the look Jude's giving her, but I can tell by the way her face quickly drops from smart ass diva, to humble and embarrassed girl. "Show me our ten most popular women's sunglasses," Jude demands.

Oh, that's right. We're in the back of the sunglass store Jude owns. I look around and notice the brands. "Of course," I say and rub my hands over my eyes.

"Of course, what?"

"Can we just get these glasses and go?"

He steps toward the door and looks out. Then comes over to me, squatting in front of me. "What did you see?"

"Um, where should I begin? Well, she has a daughter named Bella, and Bella's only a baby. She's going to try and hook up with you tonight at some club and convince you Bella is yours."

"Why would she do that?"

"Because of your money, but she's seeing some guy named Brenden."

Jude smiles and then chuckles to himself. Stevie walks in carrying a tray of sunglasses. She stops when she notices Jude laughing, and me staring at her.

"Do you wanna try them on?" she asks me rudely, though her eyes are on Jude.

"No need, we'll take all ten." He takes a money clip out of his pocket and hands her a wad of cash.

"I have to ring it up."

"We'll wait."

She takes the stack of cash and leaves again. He doesn't say a word to me the entire time she's gone. But I can tell by him scrubbing at his square jawline, and the smile on his face, that he's thinking.

She returns a couple of minutes later, and hands him his change. "Thank you," Jude says sliding his gloves back on. He grabs hold of my hand, squeezing it, and winking at me. His smug smile speaks volumes.

"Are you going to the club tonight, Jude?" she asks in her cutesy, saccharine voice.

The hair at the back of my neck stands. Nails . . . chalk board. She makes me so sick with her fakeness.

"I was considering it." Maneuvering the bag with all the sunglasses, he reaches for the door handle.

"Do I get a kiss before you go?" she asks, making me want to vomit. "Just a little kiss, Judey."

"I just threw up in my mouth," I mumble. Jude turns to me smiling. He gives me a slight wink and turns his attention to Stevie who's inched closer to him.

"Lay one on me, sugar." He turns his face, offering her his cheek.

She rises on her tiptoes to reach Jude's tall frame, and kisses him on the cheek. Her lips staying a touch too long. My skin crawls as my stomach knots. *I can't stand her.*

He pulls away and turns to me. "It might be best if you look after that baby of yours instead of trying to trick me into becoming her daddy."

All the blood drains from her face. Her cheeks pale, and her eyes widen. A small chuckle rips through me. "You okay, Stevie?" I ask, in a way to convey how I'm actually laughing *at* her.

"How . . . how did you know about her?" Stevie whispers, shocked with Jude's revelation.

"About Bella?" Jude replies. Stevie nods her head, breathless and still ghastly white. He steps closer to her, and she takes a frightened step backward. I grasp his hand, because I don't want him to hurt her. "Don't ever think you can fuck with me, Stevie."

Tears well up in her eyes. One breaks free and rolls down her cheek. She nods her head furiously, her hands by her side rolled into fists. "I'm sorry," she whispers.

We leave the store and the sound of the heavy steel door closes quite loudly. The thump makes me jump as Jude walks fast the same way we came in. "I don't like her," I say between breaths.

"Neither do I."

"But you let her kiss you." I clamp my free hand over my mouth, because I realize it makes me sound like a jealous girlfriend. Which I'm not. But her public displays of affection were sickening. Especially after I saw the vision and knew what her real intentions are . . . or were until Jude caught her out on them.

"Do I detect a hint of jealousy?"

"What?! No way." I roll my eyes at him and pretend to puke. "You're revolting." *And cute. Shut up, Lexi, he's a kidnapper and he beats people up.*

"I think you're jealous of her."

Snarling at him I say, "And I think you're delusional."

"It's okay to be jealous."

"It's okay to be delusional, too."

He laughs out loud but keeps taking me back through the corridors, and out to the concierge who handed him the electronic keycard. Jude stops at the desk, hands him the card along with a small bundle of bills and we head out through the front doors.

"I'm not entirely sure why we went this way, but it seems quite round about and a waste of time." Jude opens the car door for me, which conveniently is waiting exactly where we left it, in a 'no parking' spot. "And how did you not get a ticket?" I ask once Jude is in and the car is in motion.

"I know a lot of people."

"You still haven't told me why we went on that ridiculous detour around the world." Opening the bag, I take the first pair of glasses out and slide them on. I look to Jude who's watching me intently.

"I like them."

"Wasn't asking your opinion."

He chuckles and shakes his head. "Teenagers," he mumbles under his breath.

What's the saying? Make lemonade out of lemons? Life has given me a lemon. A six-foot-tall, dangerous, (and cute) lemon.

"How old are you?" I ask as I slide another pair of glasses on, preferring how they feel to the first pair.

He leans forward and pours himself a glass of scotch. Lifting it to his lips, he whispers, "Twenty-five," before throwing the drink back.

"You're only twenty-five?" I ask and study his face.

"Should I be insulted?"

I shrug at him. "Be whatever you want to be." I return to looking outside. The streets are getting wider, and the land rolls with breathtaking greenery, so I know we're close to Jude's house.

We pull up and I don't bother waiting for anyone to open my door. I'm out of the car with the bag of sunglasses and inside the house before Jude exits the car.

Heading up to my fortress, I notice the door's been removed and the room is completely bare.

My heart thumps wickedly against my chest, and the worse possible ideas are flashing in my mind. He's going to kill me. I know it. "Jude!" I yell.

"Everything okay?"

"First, there's no door. And second, there's no bed. And third, what's going on?" Smiling he holds his gloved hand out to me. "You're a very touchy person. You're always holding my hand. If I didn't know who you are and what you do, I'd think it was sweet and somewhat normal."

"I can be sweet, *and* I can be normal."

Dropping his hand, I refuse to go one more step without an explanation. "Jude, you don't have to try and win me over. Your threats to my family and friends ensure I'm not going anywhere."

"Duly noted, no more hand holding." He backs away, his hands high in surrender. "But I'd like for you to follow me, please."

"Is this room lined with plastic?"

He sighs loudly and shakes his head. "Just follow me."

He turns around and heads back down the stairs to the opposite side of the grand foyer. "Isn't this where your room is?" I ask, tracking behind him.

"This is where my suite is, yes. But if we continue down the hall, this is where your suite will be too."

"My suite? Why did you move me?" We keep walking down the bright corridor.

"You'll see." He stops outside a double door, smiling. "This way, if anything happens, I'll hear it."

"No guard standing outside?" I look around to see if one of his bodyguards is following stealthily behind us.

"No more guards."

"Cameras?"

He winces in pain and nods his head. "I'm afraid they're not going anywhere. However, they're no longer in the bathroom."

"You had cameras in the bathroom? You've got to be kidding me, Jude! In the bathroom?"

"I had to make sure you were safe."

"And how many of the perverted men who work for you have watched me showering? And how many of them have recorded me and shared it with their friends?"

Jude crosses his arms and leans up against the wall outside the double doors where he's stopped. "None of them. Because that camera is only seen by one person."

"Who?" I feel like slapping the stupid smirk off his face.

"Me, of course."

"You've watched me shower?" I step closer and close my fists ready to smack him.

"Highlight of my day."

I really, *really* want to lay into him. "I can't believe you," I snap as I step closer. The smug, amused look on his face makes me angrier.

"Hey, it's not my fault you're hot."

"And seventeen. And you're like thirty-nine."

"Smart ass," he mumbles. "I want to show you your new living arrangements."

"Sans cameras in the bathroom. Wait, I'll go get that ugly glove you made me wear, it'll come in handy to cover the camera in the room."

"I learned with that little stunt. I've enclosed a glass dome around the cameras." He opens the French doors and steps aside.

The first thing I notice is the size of the room. It's huge, with a large flat screen TV mounted on the wall, with shelves and shelves of movies. Diagonally opposite the TV is what looks like a reading nook. The wall is lined with books stacked both vertically and horizontally. There must be close to a thousand books carefully placed on the shelves. Opposite to it, is an art station. A large easel it set up with copious amounts of art paper, pencils, paints, and charcoal. Everything a budding artist might need.

"What is this place?" I ask as I step in and let my eyes drink every surface, every pillow, every texture in the room.

"This is your suite. You need someplace to escape to, and to make your own. If you don't like the colors I've chosen, or whatever, then let me know and I'll have it changed."

I turn to look at Jude, he shoves his hands in his pockets and lowers his chin. I get a sense of him being embarrassed. "You did this for me?"

"I didn't want you being bored. Anyway, come have a look at the rest of the suite." He walks down a corridor and peers over his shoulder to me, waiting for me to follow him. "This is the bathroom." He opens the door and I'm presented with an incredibly stunning bathroom. There's a soaking tub and a massive shower that can easily accommodate four people with numerous rainwater heads. "The floor is heated so when it's cold, you won't be."

I want to say something, to show him I appreciate what he's done for me. But the fact *he* kidnapped *me*, places him quite high on the 'dude you're a douche' registry. So, why would I thank him?

"And this is your bedroom." He opens another door off the corridor, and it leads into a room as big as the TV room and bathroom put together. The bed is in the middle of the room, a monstrosity with four heavy, carved, dark wooden columns, a thick, high headboard with a translucent white canopy draped over the top. "There's a smaller bathroom, a dressing room, and whatever entertainment you want if you prefer to stay in bed."

Walking into the dressing room, I shake my head at how

absurd this entire suite is. "This isn't a suite, Jude. This is a wing. I have everything except a damn kitchen. It's the same size as many family homes."

"Actually, there's a kitchenette too." He points to a wall. "It's a concealed kitchen. Like a butler's kitchen. Here, I'll show you." He walks to the wall, presses on a panel, which opens up to yet another extravagant room. "It'll be stocked with whatever you want. I've had the chef take note of what you enjoy and he'll be adding the foods in here."

"Am I being locked in here?"

"What? No. Why do you ask?"

"Because you're making me completely self-sufficient. Don't get me wrong, I'm okay with that, but have you got intentions on locking me in here?"

"You can come and go as you please. Anywhere in the house you want to go, go."

"Just don't leave?"

He nods his head. "Remember the choice is always yours."

I breathe in deeply and let out an exhale slowly. My choice, my ass. I have no choice in this. I leave—they die. I stay—they live.

"Is there anything else you want to show me?"

"No, that's about it," he announces proudly.

"Great. I need pads and tampons. I'll have my period next week and I need them unless you want my blood everywhere." He shudders and frowns in disgust. "Thought so. Can you make sure I have them?"

"I'll make sure to get you what you need. Anything else?" I shake my head. The air between us becomes heavy. I no longer want to see him. I want to be left alone. "I should go then." He hesitates, hanging back, waiting for something. But he's going to get nothing from me. Slowly he walks out of my room, and toward the front door of the suite. "You can lock the door from the inside, only I have the key." I don't bother responding. Instead, I use all my will to hold back the tears.

I miss my family so much.

"I'll be in my office if you need me."

Keeping it together, I muster the strength to nod my head and offer him a fake smile. He walks slowly, waiting for me to talk.

I have nothing nice to say.

My heart is aching, screaming at me to run as fast as I can and get to my parents before he realizes I'm even gone. But a man like Jude would know I was gone within a second of me leaving the grounds.

And my parents would be assassinated before I had the chance to reach them.

"I'll be in my office," he says again before resigning himself to the fact that I'm remaining mute. *By choice.* I don't want to talk to him anymore.

The moment he's out in the corridor, I close the door and lock it from the inside. Fruitless, considering he has a key. But we both know I don't want him here.

I take myself to my new room, climb on top of the imposing bed, and hug one of the pillows. The tears break free, and I'm absolutely devastated at this thing called life. Life sucks.

Jude may be treating me well, but it doesn't mean I want to be here.

The stupid tears keep coming, and they don't want to stop. The heaviness in my heart and body crushes every morsel of hope. The air becomes dense with hopelessness. There's nothing I can do to get out of here.

My head clouds with more sadness, and my eyes become droopy. The tears finally stop just as my mind blanks and I fall asleep.

CHAPTER 17

IT'S BEEN TWELVE days since Jude showed me to my new living quarters. He's been hanging around a lot, and I've been crying even more. I hold it together when he's around, but once I'm back in my room, I lose it.

Guilt floods me, while my broken heart keeps beating.

The nights are worse than the days, because it's when I miss my parents the most. The sorrow makes me feel weak and pathetic with the constant tears I've been shedding.

There's a knock on the door, and I yell out for whoever it is to come in. The only person it can be is Jude, all the guards are under strict instruction to not disturb me.

"Dinner's ready," Jude announces as he casually sits on the bed. "You coming out to eat?"

"Sure." I feel so lost and overwhelmed by sadness. But I have to try and keep going, hoping against hope Jude will let me go home.

"I'm taking you somewhere after dinner."

"Okay," I reply in a monotone voice. "Is it work related?"

"No, it's not. I know how much you're struggling with being here."

I turn over on the bed so he can't see me, and let another tear fall. I try to steady my voice before I say, "I'll be fine."

I hear Jude's heavy steps as he leaves my room. "I'll wait for you for dinner." The door clicks shut and I know he's gone.

With my heavy heart, and my teary eyes, I drag myself out of bed and head out toward the kitchen. The smell of spices wafts through the house from the moment I leave my suite. My stomach growls in anticipation of what the chef's prepared.

Walking into the kitchen, I see Jude's standing at the end of the table talking on his phone. As soon as his eyes land on me, he whispers something into the phone.

This house is filled with secrets. I suppose if you're a criminal, you'd have to keep everything close to your chest and not let people in.

"I have to go," he says as I get closer to him. There's no need in asking him who he's on the phone with, because it's none of my business. "Are you hungry?" he asks, pulling the chair out for me to sit.

"Yeah, starving." Jude sits, and Frank brings over two plates with cutlery. "Thank you, Frank." Frank may be old, but since I've been here I've come to learn a few things about him. His wife Janet passed away, and he's lonely, but I learned that through the first vision Jude tested me on. I've also learned how Frank's only son passed away years ago from a rare form of cancer, and Jude paid for all his medical costs.

"You're welcome, Miss Lexi," Frank responds.

"Please, just Lexi." I hate how he calls me 'miss.' To me, it feels wrong. He's so much older than me; it almost feels disrespectful.

"Yes, Miss Lexi," he replies.

He moves to the other side of the kitchen, and brings a dish to the table. He starts piling food on our plates. Jude watches him, and when our plates are stacked high, Frank leaves the kitchen.

Picking my fork up, I taste what Frank's made. Of course, it's beautiful, like everything else he makes for me.

"How are you feeling?" Jude asks between forkfuls of food.

"Don't ask questions you really don't want an answer to. Just get to whatever it is you want to know."

He smiles, and continues eating. "You always cut to the chase, don't you? I want to get a better understanding of your ability."

"I'll give you one when I work it out for myself."

"You have to know something about it. When did you first realize you had it?"

Tilting my head to the side, I narrow my eyes at him. "You did all this research on me, and found out so many things, and you have no idea when it started?

"Feisty today. I like it."

God, he pisses me off so much. "After I had my operation."

"For your appendicitis?"

"You know about that?"

"I have your hospital records, so yes, I know about that."

"Stalker much?" He laughs and keeps inhaling his food as if he'll never eat again. "Slow down, Jude, you'll give yourself indigestion." He waves me away and keeps cramming more food into his mouth. "Anyway, it started when I woke after the operation. A nurse . . ." I drift off remembering Hayley, and how she died. My skin prickles as a cold chill clampers my spine.

"What nurse?" His voice makes me stare at him, and leave the memory of Hayley.

"Hayley. She had a pink bow in her long, dark hair. And the kindest eyes. She was so sweet to me, but she was killed by a man with a scar running down his face." I point to my cheek.

"Did you see a vision?"

I nod my head and place my fork on the side of the plate. "I saw a vision of the man who killed her. He knew her, because after he shot her he stood over her body and said 'you should've listened to me.' I've never been more frightened in my life. I had no idea what was going on; until I saw on the news how she'd been shot. And while I was watching it, it was like déjà vu, and I couldn't stop it. I couldn't even tell anyone, because I was so afraid they'd think I was losing my mind. I should've said something to her." Heaviness circles my heart, and I place my hand on my chest to rub it away. More shame creeps in because I could've saved her, *but I didn't*.

Jude moves his chair closer to me, and rubs circles on my back. "If you had told her, she wouldn't have believed you."

Burying my face into my hands, an overwhelming sense of guilt takes my body hostage. "I could've saved her. I should've said something. I'm kicking myself that I held it in and didn't tell her. But I really had no idea what was going on. It's why . . ." I look up at Jude, staring into his dangerous eyes.

"It's why what?" When he narrows his eyes in question, a deep crease appears between them.

"It's why, when I saw what happened to you — or was going to happen – I had to warn you. I promised myself, no matter how crazy it might sound, I had to make sure you knew not to go to the dock."

"I'm forever indebted to you for telling me."

"Hah," I chuckle bitterly and look away from him. "And this is how you repay me?" I sigh in frustration.

"Lexi, you're too valuable to not explore how your gift works."

"Let's agree to disagree. Anyway, what made you believe me instead of thinking I was insane?" He frowns at me again. "I mean, why did you believe me?"

His lips turn up in a smile. "My mom used to tell me of a witch her mother knew back in the village where they lived."

"Village?"

"My grandparents came from France."

"France?" This shocks me. I was expecting him to say either Italy or Russia. He has dark coloration, dark eyes, dark hair, even an olive skin tone. I never would've taken him for having French heritage.

"Yeah, France, why do you sound so shocked? Don't tell me, you group people in my line of work as Italian . . . perhaps Russian?"

My face floods with color, and I'm embarrassed to admit it. "Yeah."

"Stereotyping, are you? France is one of the most profitable hubs for underworld activities because it draws from neighboring countries for drugs, girls and guns."

"Wow," I whisper, genuinely shocked to learn this. Bile rises to the back of my throat when he says 'girls.' How sickening.

"As I was saying, my grandparents lived in France, in a remote village, and my mom told me of a witch who could foresee the future simply by reading a person's palm. My mother never believed her, until the witch grabbed hold of my mom's hand when she was fifteen and told her of a man who was going to pass through the village. This man was considerably older, and he had a young son, slightly older than my mother. The man was going to try to rape my mother and his son was going to kill him."

"Whoa. So much darkness and horror." I listen intently as Jude continues the story of the old lady, his mother, and the men passing through.

"Sure enough, three days later an older man and his son were passing through and asked for a place to spend the night. My mother's parents, being good farm people, opened their home and invited the man and his son in."

Stunned, and with my mouth open, I sit staring at Jude, lost in his story. I'm so drawn in to listening to this tale that I can't help but lean in, glued to Jude.

"My grandfather sent my mother out to the farm to do some small job, and the man followed her out. He tried to rape her. His son saw this, and he was infatuated by my mother. He hit his father over the head with a shovel to get him off her, but the force of the hit cracked his skull and killed him instantly."

"Your mother told you this?" Jude nods his head. "And you believe it?"

He sits back, shocked that I'm even questioning it. "Why wouldn't I?"

"I mean, if we were reading this in a book, or watching a movie we'd both be saying this is a load of shit."

"This ain't no movie, and definitely no book. Look at you, you have the ability to see a person's future when you touch them. Nothing made up about you or your gift."

"In a world where everything is supposed to be black or white, I have to accept there's so many variants of color in between. Makes me wonder what else in life is true." I run my hand over my eyebrows and try to focus on what we're talking about now, instead of going off in a tangent. "But what happened with your mom and the boy who killed his father?"

"They left the village, and came here."

"Wait, the boy who saved your mom became your dad?" He nods his head. "And they moved here?" He nods again, but this time adds a smile. "Why didn't they stay there?"

"Because they thought no one would believe his father was trying to rape my mother. They decided to leave, and never go back. They thought it was their only option. To disappear."

"Did they ever return to France?"

"Nope. Once they came here, they got married and lived their life."

He takes a deep breath and continues eating what's left on his plate. "How did your dad get into . . . you know, the business?" Even saying it aloud sounds stupid. 'The business,' sounds illicit and mysterious, and dumb.

"He killed another man."

"After his father?" Jude nods. Looking past Jude, I'm trying to not focus on the obvious, that Jude has been brought up in a family where killing was okay. That must really mess with a person's head. "Do I want to know?" I finally ask, breaking the restless tension in the air.

"You know what, Lexi." He abruptly stands. "I don't think you do. It's stuff nightmares are made of. Actually, it's stuff the nightmares are afraid of. So no, I won't tell you anymore. You don't need to know." There's something behind his tone. It's dripping with remorse, and another emotion I can't quite put my finger on. It's almost like he's trying to protect me from the ghosts of his past.

Picking my fork up, I manage to eat two more bites before Frank appears and clears the table. "Do I get to finish?" I ask while Frank's halfway across the kitchen with my plate.

"I promised to take you out. So, let's go."

"But . . ." I follow Frank with my eyes and pout to Jude.

"Trust me on this one, you'll enjoy it."

"Fine," I groan as I stand. "Are you going to tell me where we're going?"

"And spoil the surprise? Never."

Of course not. We head out of the kitchen, and I call to Frank, "Thanks for dinner, Frank."

"You're welcome, Miss Lexi," Frank replies. He's a nice man; I like him.

When we get to the front door, the guard opens it and stands to the side. The limousine is waiting for us, and the replacement driver has the back door open. "What happened with the other driver?"

Jude peers over at me, his eye brows flying up high. "Do you want an honest answer?"

Ugh, not now. "I'm good." I shake my head. With his response, I'm fairly sure I already know the answer. I don't need to hear it to confirm what I'm thinking.

"Tell me something about you, Lexi."

"Don't you have everything you need to know on file in your office, locked in the safe?"

"You know about the safe?" he asks with a hint of worry.

I swing my head around to look at him. And this time, it's me who's thinking he's a dumb-ass. "Now I do. But it's obvious to me, that a man like yourself, in your line of work, would have a safe. So yes, I know there'll be a safe, somewhere, and likely there'll be several of them." The amused look in his eyes makes his entire face light up. "Thought so," I add.

"Considering you know about the safe, or safes, which I won't confirm, I'll answer your question. Yes, I have a file on you, and yes, it's locked in one of my safes."

My mouth falls open and I feel like smacking my head. He just established two things. One: the fact he has multiple safes, and two: he has a file on me. "What's the something you want to know?"

"Do you have a boyfriend?"

The question is surprising, and totally not any of his business. "Why, would you kidnap him so we'd be living together in your house?"

Jude's face falters, his eyes narrow and he clenches his jaw together tightly. His Adam's apple bobs up and down as he swallows. I notice how his hands ball together into tight fists. "Do you have one, or not, Lexi?"

"None of your damn business, *Jude*. Anyway, who cares if I did or didn't, because I'm never going to see him again," my voice rises along with the anger simmering away inside me.

"Damn right you're not going to see him again. But, who is he?"

"I'm not telling you shit, you have no reason to know."

"Like hell I don't."

My blood is now boiling with rage. How dare he demand to know. "None of your damn business," I say with an eerily calm voice. My placid tone is definitely not a reflection of the fury he's inviting.

"Alexa." He wraps his fingers around my upper arm, and tugs me back toward him.

I look at his hand and see how he's carefully sheathed his fingers with the fabric of my t-shirt. "I'm not telling you."

He drops his hand, but not before applying a bit too much pressure around my upper arm. Squeezing . . . warning me. He scrubs his hand over his face, and huffs a few times. "Please, I'd like to know if you have a boyfriend?" this time his voice is calm.

"That's better. I prefer this tone to the angry one. But it's still none of your damn business. Don't expect an answer."

"For fuck's sake!" he yells.

I flinch at his outburst. But I straighten my shoulders and hold my head high. I refuse to tell him, even though doing so would be much easier. I won't give him this part of me. He doesn't need to know.

Looking out the window, I can't see much. It's too dark outside. I take this time, and the extreme silence in the car to calm down and not react to him. He's an idiot if he thinks I'm going to answer the question.

Before long, my blood pressure settles and my rapid breathing returns to normal. Still looking out the window, I notice the surroundings. "Where are we, Jude?" I sit up straighter in the back seat and stare as we approach my home.

"You know where we are."

"Are you going to let me see my parents? Am I free?" I ask with so much hope in my voice. My body is buzzing with excitement. He's letting me go. *I'm free.* My shoulders shake with enthusiasm as I stare out the window. Bursting with elation at finally seeing them again. It's been weeks since he took me.

The silence in the car screams at me.

Something's not right.

Turning to look at Jude, I see the seriousness on his face. He shakes his head at me, and my heart tears into two. "No, I'm not letting you go."

Sorrow dampens every ounce of excitement. A blanket of hurt wraps around my body. My shoulders slump, and heart falls into the pit of my stomach. "Are you going to kill them? Please don't, I'll do better. I promise, I'll stop talking back. Please, Jude, please don't kill them." Tears leak out of my eyes, as I launch myself at him. "I don't have a boyfriend, I never wanted one. Please, see I'm trying, please," I shamelessly beg.

"I'm not going to kill them."

I move away from him, sitting back in my seat. The sobs give way to just light tears. "Then why did you bring me here?"

"I know how sad you've been, Lexi, and I thought this might ease the pain."

We pull up opposite my house. It's dark outside, but I can see the house so clearly. My heart hurts. I want to run up the front path, fling the door open and hurl myself in the arms of my parents. Jude knocks on the glass, and a moment later someone walks up to Dad's car, which is parked in the street, and swings a baseball bat at the headlight.

"What's he doing?" I place my hand on the handle, ready to push the door open and go run after the guy.

Jude stops me by grabbing hold of the back of my t-shirt, preventing me from leaving the car.

The guy runs off, and within seconds a car takes off past us. I recognize the car as one of Jude's. The light on the porch comes on, the door flies open and Dad bounds outside. "Daddy," I cry, seeing him in his pajamas. Placing my hand on the window, I watch as Mom follows seconds later. "Mommy," I whisper.

They both look like they've aged decades. They've lost so much weight, and even though it's dark and I'm not close to them, I can still see the dark circles beneath their eyes. They look so sad, and so lost.

My heart breaks even more seeing them as close as they are, but unable to go to them and give them a hug. Dad looks down the street, then up and then directly at the car. "Daddy." More tears fall. "Please, Jude, let me have one more hug. Just one more word," I beg. "Please." I don't dare look at Jude, because I want to soak my parents up. I want to stare at them for as long as I can before they leave to go back inside.

"I'm sorry, Alexa, I can't."

"Please?" I beg fruitlessly. I can't have one more hug and leave again. I'd embrace them and never let them go. "I'll do anything you want, I just need them to see I'm okay and stop worrying for me. Please, Jude, please."

Dad turns to look at Mom, and they both head back inside.

Where's Marcus or Laura? Why aren't they protecting my parents?

I beg again, this time through heavy sobs. I bash on the window, calling for my parents who are now inside the house.

Jude knocks on the glass divider and the car rolls away quietly.

"Why did you bring me here?" I ask. Venom spilling from my mouth. Hatred filling my veins.

"I can't let you go, Lexi, but I wanted you to see your parents. It's the best I can do for you."

I blink the tears away, and compose myself. Turning, I look at Jude. "I've never hated you more than I do right now. You gave me a glimpse of what my life could be, and then you rip it away like you don't care at all."

"Problem is, I do care."

"You have a funny way of showing it." I turn back and close my eyes, containing the tears that want to fall. "Never bring me here again."

It completely destroys my heart to think of never seeing my parents again. But it's what I have to do to make sure I survive through this, and that they survive too.

My heart is broken, and now my soul is too.

CHAPTER 18

I CRIED THE night we came back from seeing my parents. Like an arrow directly to my heart, it created such a gaping hole that I don't think it'll ever mend.

I cried the next day too, and refused to leave my prison.

And I cried the next day.

But it was on the third day of me crying, that I decided I had to do exactly whatever it was in order to survive. And that meant I had to pull my shoulders back, stop crying, and harness this gift I was given.

I spent the entire day yesterday trying to figure out how it works. But considering it didn't come with an instruction manual, all I got was frustrated.

Today, I'm going to attempt to understand this ability more comprehensively. Jumping out of bed with a new-found mission, I change into a t-shirt and shorts and head out into the kitchen.

Jude looks up from his tablet and smiles at me. "Good morning. You're up early," he says as he watches me.

I've made a vow to myself, I'm going to master this thing I have, and I'm going to use it for my own personal gain. Not Jude's and not anyone else's.

"I am." Frank walks over and places a mug down. "Thank you, Frank." I gently place my hand on his and I'm instantly in his home.

He's staring up at the wedding photo of him and Janet, and he's nursing a cup of something. "She talked to me today, sweetheart," he says to his wife. "She came out of her room, and she wasn't crying. That made my day."

"Aww, you're so beautiful," I say as I stand beside him.

Frank's head whips to the side as he drops the mug he's holding. "Is there someone here?" he calls out while looking directly at me, without knowing I'm here.

I take a few deep breaths, and try to shuffle forward so I'm standing nearly nose to nose with him. "Can you hear me, Frank?"

"Hello?"

He can obviously hear something, because he's responding to me. I close my eyes and calm my erratic heartbeat.

Taking deep breaths, I pour all my focus into moving closer to him, and him hearing me. Opening my eyes, I stare at Frank, whose face has drained of color. His eyes are wide with fear, and he's holding onto the mantel below the picture of him and his wife.

"Frank," I say.

"Hello? Who's there?"

My skin sparks alive, as the hair on the back of my neck stands to attention. "Frank, can you hear me?"

"Janet? Janet, sweetheart." Tears pour down his cheeks as he tries to identify the source of the sound. "Is it my time to come to you? Please tell me it is."

"Frank, it's Lexi."

Frank's shaking his head while still looking in my direction. He rubs his hands over his eyes, and then his ears. "Sweetheart, it's okay if you've come for me. I'm ready, really I am."

Reaching out to touch him, I'm transported back into the kitchen.

But this time, I'm on the ground, being cradled by Jude.

"What happened?" I ask drowsily as I try and stand. My head is spinning, and I feel like I'm about to throw up.

"Are you okay?" Jude asks.

Trying to get my bearings, I look around the kitchen. Frank has the most astounded look on his pale face. His eyes are like small slits with his bushy brows drawn together.

Jude stands and picks me up, like I'm his bride and walks me toward my room. "What happened back there, Lexi?"

Looking down at his arms, I see he's wearing a long-sleeved shirt, his hands covered with black leather gloves. "I'm not sure."

"What did you do?" he asks in a calm voice. "You grabbed hold of Frank's hand, and within seconds your eyes rolled into the back of your head and you began having a seizure."

"What?" Is this why my head feels fuzzy?

"What are you trying to do? Why did you grab hold of his hand?" He opens the door to my suite, then walks me into my bedroom, where he gently places me on my bed. I crawl up the bed, and hug my knees. He goes into the kitchen area, where I hear the tap running. A few seconds pass before he brings over a glass of water. "Here, drink this."

Hesitantly I reach out to grab the glass and have a small mouthful. "Thank you."

He sits on the end of the bed, and links his gloved hands together. "What are you doing?"

The fuzziness in my head begins to lift, and I look down at the glass encased in my hands. "I'm finding it hard to be here. Especially after you took me to see my parents."

He nods his head and leans his elbow on his knee. "It was a mistake for me to take you there. It won't happen again."

"It can't happen again, Jude. I'm trying to learn to survive in your world, and flaunting my parents to me without letting me talk to them or hug them, sucks and it hurts. It hurts so much, that the only way I can get through it is if I can master what this thing I have is, so I know how to use it properly."

"And what happened with Frank?"

"I spoke to him, and he heard me."

"He heard you?" His brows fly up and his eyes widen with surprise. "You talked to him?"

"He didn't know it was me, he thought it was Janet, but he could hear something. It happened the day with Stevie too. She heard something. But I need to practice so I can get more control over it. It'll help me understand what I'm capable of."

"Not at the risk of your health. You scared the shit out of me."

"At the risk of my health?" I sit up straighter and place the glass on the table beside the bed. "You think it's healthier for me to be here rather than back at home with my parents?'

"I can protect you here." He abruptly stands and walks over to one of the two huge, and unbreakable windows in the room.

"You think I'm better off here than with my parents? My own flesh and blood who'll do anything to keep me safe?"

"Anyone can get to you at your parents' house. Here, you're protected. Even with the bodyguards your parents hired, I got to you, which means anyone can get to them."

"No one else knows about this thing I have going on inside my head. Only you and I." I jump off the bed and follow him over to the window, ready for a heated argument.

"And this is where you're showing your naivety, Lexi."

"I'm not naïve."

He steps closer, places his hands on my shoulders and smiles at me. "This thing you have, it didn't appear out of thin air. It was placed inside you, more than likely when you went in for the operation you had. Someone, somewhere knows you have it, and that means one day, they will try to come and collect what's theirs."

I take a small step backward. I never thought of it like that. Never considered for even one moment, didn't entertain the thought, that this 'gift' was deliberately put inside me by someone. "Jude, this means they'll go after my parents." I grab hold of his arms, and squeeze. "Please, you can't let anything happen to them."

"I've got my people looking out for them."

It dawns on me, how he can play a critical role, either way for me. I leave, his people will get the green light to kill them. I stay, his people will be under instruction to protect them. "What happens when your people stop listening to you?" Fear encompasses everything within me. There's a very real possibility, that someday my parents will be killed, because of me.

Jude tilts his head to the side, shocked by my question. "My people always listen to me. And if they don't, they know what the consequences will be."

"Jude, you have to promise me you'll do everything you can to protect them."

"My only concern is you and your safety. Nothing else matters to me."

Suddenly, my body reacts to his words. Why is he so damn protective of me? "What aren't you telling me?" I ask.

His severely dark eyes hold my stare for a second before he turns his head away from me. "My concern is you, Lexi. Only you."

What does he mean? "You frustrate me." Running my hand through my hair, I massage the nape of my neck. "Just . . . please, I've done everything you've wanted me to, all I ask is you protect them."

He reluctantly nods his head while still looking outside.

Relief floods me. An overwhelming sense of relief wipes out the worry. Stepping forward, I move into his personal space and hug him. He's my captor, but at least he's going to protect the people who matter most to me. "Thank you," I whisper as I lean my head onto his chest.

Both of us lose ourselves for a split second. His lips touch my forehead, and I'm standing in an isolated, stark though well-lit room. Looking around, Jude's standing in front of a man who's sitting on a chair.

The man is dressed in a white, blood-splotched t-shirt, and his jeans are covered with blood splatters too.

"Where am I?"

Jude turns his body in my direction. I notice he has metal rings on his right hand, which are covered in blood. The head of the man on the chair is slumped, but I can see his shoulders rising and falling rapidly.

Jude steps in front of the body, like he's shielding me from the blood and gore. But it's too late, I've already seen what he's done. "What are you doing?" I ask.

Jude steps forward, as if he can see me. "You need to leave," he tells me.

Looking around the room, I see a surgical trolley beside the man. There are implements on the trolley that don't appear to be of surgical grade.

Pliers.

Rope.

A manual saw.

A utility knife.

It doesn't take a genius to know what's been happening, and what's about to happen in this room.

I'm back in my room, and Jude gently grabs me by my shoulders and moves me back. I look down at his hands and wonder how something so soft on me, can cause so much devastation. "How can you do it?" I ask.

"What did you see?"

"You. You're going to kill him, right?"

He doesn't even try to deny it, or even lie. "Yes."

"Why?"

"He stole from me. He needs to die."

I suck in a breath and avert my eyes from him. Stepping back, I try and push the images of the man Jude was hurting as far away as possible. "I know it's naive of me, but I don't want to know."

There's an awkward silence before Jude starts to speak again. "Tell me about the guy you saw who killed the nurse."

A shiver of ice rips through me as the memory of Hayley being killed becomes vibrant. "He had a scar, like this down his cheek." I point to my face and indicate how the scar was positioned. "He was wearing a hoodie. Even though he looked at me, I can't describe him very clearly. His face should be burnt into my memory, but the night I saw him I was doped high on drugs the hospital had given me. "The only thing I can tell you is that he's young, around the same age as Hayley. But he knew her."

Jude takes his phone out of his pocket and walks toward my front door. He dials someone while watching me. "Find me everything you can on a nurse who was killed a couple of months ago. Her first name was Hayley. Hang on." He lowers the phone so it's against his leg, looks at me and asks, "Where did she die?"

"It was at the train station, close to the hospital where I had my operation."

He brings the phone up to his ear, and begins to talk in a soft voice so I can't hear him. When he's finished, he places the phone back in his pocket and returns to me. "Will you be okay tonight? I have some work to do."

I'm confused and bewildered. "Seriously? I know exactly what you're going to do."

"It's work."

"Why did you want to know about the guy who killed Hayley?"

Now it's his turn to look at me in a way that says. 'Come on, Lexi, you know exactly why.' "Seriously?" he repeats my word back to me.

"You should let the authorities find him."

"I have no faith in the justice system."

"Hey, my mom is a damn good judge."

He holds his hands up, then sits in one of the armchairs in my room. I sit on my bed, and cross my legs. "Your mom is a damn good judge. And an honest one too. But let me tell you something. There's so much work the cops have to do before the case even gets in front of your mom. Most criminals aren't caught."

I start to chuckle, then cough. "Present company included."

"I have no idea what you're talking about," he replies coldly.

"You really should let the police do their work and have him prosecuted."

"Do you know why I'm doing this?" I shake my head. "Because I know this is important to you. You saw something you can never unsee. He took a life he didn't deserve to take, so I'll make sure he can never hurt anyone again."

"And who are you to play God and decide when he should die?"

"Usually I don't give a shit. But it's important to you to make sure this guy is found. I'll find him, Lexi, I promise you that. But I'll be taking care of it, the way I know how to."

"But then I'm shouldering more of the responsibility because I know what you're going to do to him."

"You have nothing to do with it, because you don't control me. I'll never bring you anywhere you can see anything."

I let out a humorless chuckle. "Problem is, Jude, every time I touch you, I'm exactly where you're going to be, and I see *exactly* what you're doing. I see everything."

Jude responds with his own humorless chuckle. "And if you tried to explain it to a judge, they wouldn't believe you. They'd think you'd lost your mind."

This angers me, because *he* believes me, which means in today's day and age, I'm sure others would too. But then if that's true, why didn't I speak out much sooner and save Hayley's life? Because, deep down inside, I know Jude's right. No one will believe me. Hell, if Dallas told me she had this gift, *this power,* I'd think she was delusional.

I'm stuck in a conundrum. I know Jude will find him. He's a

man who has demonstrated how proficient he is. He's also shown me the persona he adopts when he's in that zone. I want the guy who killed Hayley to be dealt with, but the only choice I have is to let Jude take care of him.

"This is too much for me, Jude." Grabbing my head, I flex my fingers and try to angrily massage my scalp.

"You have nothing to worry about." I hear him stand, and the bed dips beside me. "I promise you, Alexa, I'll never let anything happen to you." He rubs gentle circles on my back. His touch is welcomed.

"You're forcing me to accept what you do, which goes against everything I've been taught by my parents. It's too much for me to handle." Looking up at him, I notice his eyes have softened. They aren't as hard as they normally are, there's no anger or dominance behind them.

He whispers words I already know. "I can't let you go." But this time, the words seem to have a different meaning to them.

"I know," I reply with a small frown. The silence between us is weighted with strain. "I know I have to accept my life as it is now, and move forward with the hope you keep your word and watch out for my parents." So much is riding heavy on my shoulders. It literally feels like my body is crumbling under such a burden.

"You have my word."

He now needs to prove it to me. I nod my head and opt to remain silent.

It's a long few minutes before he speaks again. "I have work to do tonight, so I won't be around. Do you need anything?" I shake my head, still quiet. I saw the 'work' he had to do tonight. "And, I have some work out of town that I have to tend to."

Swinging around, I look into his eyes. The softness has been replaced with his usual cold hardness. "Okay," I say.

"I leave in two days, and I'll be gone for no longer than three days. Everyone here has been briefed on their role with you."

I frown at him, suddenly feeling like I'm his pet project. I suppose I am. "And what exactly have you told them?" my voice comes out snappy, and pissed off.

He tries to contain his smirk, but I catch the edge of his mouth move upward before he notices. "Whatever you need, they're under instructions to get it for you. Frank will be staying here for those nights, so if you want to talk to someone, he's here."

"And the rest of your people?"

"Know if anything happens to you, I'll kill each and every one of them."

I sigh a deep breath and look forward. I exhale again and know he means what he's said. "I won't ask what you'll be doing."

"I won't tell you even if you ask."

His reply makes me smile. At least he's truthful. "Tell me something?"

"Anything."

"Is there honor among thieves, or is it each man for himself?"

He chuckles for a second, then answers, "There's no such thing as honor among thieves. It's each man for himself. I could have dinner with an associate one night, then rat him out the next. It's all about survival, I do what I need to do in order to survive."

"Then why should I believe that you'll look after me and I won't end up like one of your associates?"

He narrows his eyes at me. I've asked a hard question. "Because you're different."

I don't ask how I'm different, because at this stage I don't want to know.

CHAPTER 19

Jude left for his out-of-town business yesterday. Other than Frank, no one else has talked to me. The guards pass me and give me a curt nod, but no words are exchanged.

"Miss Lexi, are you okay?" Frank asks me as I sit in the kitchen for breakfast.

"I'm okay, how are you?"

"My day is always better when I see you hungry and wanting to eat." He smiles at me, and brings me over a stack of pancakes.

"These look great. I don't like eating alone. Would you care to join me?" I like Frank; he always makes me smile.

"I've already eaten this morning, Miss Lexi. If I have too much more, I'm afraid it'll spoil my youthful good looks and rocking hard body." He pats his stomach then flexes his arm muscles making me laugh. "But I will have coffee with you." Walking over to the coffee machine, he makes one for himself, and a hot chocolate for me. "Here you go." He places my mug in front of me, and sits opposite me.

"How long have you worked for Jude?' I ask as I slice into the stack of fluffy, delicious pancakes. I grumble an appreciative moan which makes Frank laugh.

"Good, are they?"

"Mmm," I reply, my mouth full.

Frank's moustache has coffee drops in it and I can't help but smile at them. He begins to tell me his story, more about his wife Janet. "She is the love of my life, there's been no one since her. No one else can compare to what I had with her."

I already know this, I can feel the love in his heart when he talks about her, and I can even feel it the few times I've been in a vision with him. "How did she die?" I know their son passed away from cancer, but I don't know about his wife.

"She passed away too early. She had a stroke, and by the time I got her to the hospital, she was gone."

"Oh, I'm sorry, Frank."

He looks at the mug between his big hands, and smiles. Tears well up in his eyes, and he tries his best to contain them. For a man of his age, it must be difficult to talk candidly and be so open with someone he barely knows. But it would be even harder for him to show emotion. Men of his generation didn't do feelings. They kept it bottled up and refused to show any type of emotion.

"It was hard when Samuel passed away. Jude was at the hospital when Samuel got sick." He smiles as he recalls the day. I can't imagine what he'd be smiling at. "He heard me trying to make a payment arrangement with the hospital for Samuel. I had no health care, and Samuel had exhausted his. Jude was my guardian angel. I still have no idea why he helped me."

This is intriguing. Why would Jude help Frank? "And you didn't know Jude?"

He chuckles and looks at me. "I don't live under a rock, Miss Lexi. I knew exactly who he was when he stepped forward and told the nurse to charge it to him."

"What happened next?"

"He told me he needed a chef because his last one didn't work out."

A chill rips up my spine, and my shoulders shudder in response. Both Frank and I know exactly what it means when Jude speaks those words. "Oh," I respond.

"I've been here going on five years now, Miss Lexi, and he

looks after me like I'm his own flesh and blood. I keep my nose out of all his business."

"Oh," I say again, not really sure how to respond to him.

"Even his lady friends, they don't last long. A night or two."

"Ugh." Grimacing, my pancakes suddenly taste sour. "It's not my business either." But the knot in my stomach and bad taste in my mouth tells a different story.

"This house was always so cold. Now, I see a difference in him. He's . . ." I lift my head to see Frank smiling. " . . . different."

"How?"

He furrows his brows together, then takes a sip of his coffee. "I think you've made an impact on him."

"Me?" I almost screech. "I haven't done anything."

He shakes his head. "Well, whatever you haven't done, keep not doing it." He chuckles again.

Suddenly, one of the guards comes running into the kitchen. "COPS!" he yells at the top of his lungs.

Stunned, Frank doesn't respond. "What?" I ask with panic starting to climb.

"Cops!"

Frank leaps out of his chair, accidently knocking the coffee cup over. Like slow motion, the contents spill all over the table. He lurches forward, grabbing me by my shoulder, pulling me to my feet and pushing me behind him.

"What's happening?" I question as I watch men in vests with big letters spelling 'POLICE' on the front and back yell commands.

"Get down!"

"Where's Jude Caley?"

"Lay on the ground."

"Hands behind your head."

A heap of demands are being shouted, so many people are scrambling. My body shakes with fear as more and more people yell.

"Get down, now!"

I drop to the ground, and someone lays a knee into my lower back.

"Don't touch her!" I hear someone yell. I want to look up, but I'm too terrified of what I might see. The voice is familiar. A female voice, but I can't quite place it.

"It'll be okay, Miss Lexi. Just be quiet and don't say anything. Mr. Jude will get us out of this," Frank whispers from beside me.

I'm too frightened to respond to him. I don't know what's going on, or who these people are. I mean, the guard said they're cops, but other than that, I don't know what department they're from. Looking at Frank, his eyes are filled with worry, and his face shows every day of his age. The lines etched across his forehead seem deeper, even though his words are trying to calm me.

"Hands behind your back," a man says to me and nudges me with his foot. I do exactly what he says. The cold, sharp sting of handcuffs encircles my wrists. Closing my eyes, I try to get a vision of who's touching me. But I'm getting nothing.

"Cuff him too," the female voice announces. The 'him' she's referring to must be Frank. Opening my eyes, I'm just in time to see Frank being tugged up and led out of my sight.

I'm jerked up roughly and dragged to my feet before they push me through the kitchen out to the main foyer. "Where are you taking me?" I get pushed again, and this time I stumble over my own feet from the force of the shove. Falling forward, someone behind me grabs hold of the cuffs and tugs me back into an upright position, causing a sharp pain to sear through my wrists. "Where am I going?" I yell and get no response.

This is my opportunity to leave Jude and go back home. The opportunity I've been searching for.

"In the van," a man says from behind me. I turn to look at him, but he's unfamiliar to me. As I approach the black van, with heavily tinted windows, I try to look around and take note of everything going on.

The guy helps me in the van and the moment he touches me, I try and get into his vision, but I'm not getting anything. I twist behind me to look at where he's holding me and notice his bare skin on mine.

I'm not getting a vision, though. Why can't I see anything?

Is it the stress, the worry over what's happening?

As I get pushed onto a bench seat, I think back to all my visions. The first one I had when I was in the hospital came to me while I was under extreme duress. I had no idea what was happening to me, but they continued to come. I was stressing out and thought I was losing my mind. But they still kept coming.

But since I'm learning more about it, all my visions have come to me while I've been calm, and in control of myself. The more in control I am, the clearer the vision, and the more detail I can get.

"Lean forward," the guy who pushed me into the van says.

Calming my heart rate, I try to still my mind. To clear it of the panic and stress, I focus on numbing myself so I can get into a vision.

The guy touches my hands again, and I'm ripped into a vision, but I'm there for only a second before I'm kicked out. *Come on, Lexi, calm down.* Closing my eyes, I take several deep breaths. I need to see what's happening, and who these people are. I feel his hands fumbling around mine, and hear the door slide shut of the van. The motion of the van jolts me forward, and more of his hands go on my wrists. The guy is uncuffing me, his hand touches mine.

I'm back in the vision. He's sitting in an office; his head is down as he reads over paperwork. I try to step forward, but my legs are weighted and I can't move. Now is not the time for this to fail me. I need to see more, I need to learn more.

Move your damn legs.

I shuffle forward. Looking at the paperwork, I gather everything I have inside me, evoking all my strength to move forward.

And just like that, a major roadblock lifts from inside of me. I move around freely, I see clearer, I smell everything. I'm in this vision and it's the clearest it's ever been.

Walking around to where this guy is pouring his energy into the paperwork, I lean down to get a better look at what he's studying.

The connection is lost, and I'm back in the van. It's traveling at a reasonable speed, and I try to look out the front window to get a sense of any landmarks.

"Where are we going?" I ask the guy beside me. Looking at my left hand, it's handcuffed to a bar which is attached to the van. Essentially, I'm stuck to the interior of the van. "Where are we going?"

The man blinks at me, then stares forward, not answering my question.

"What's happening?" Other than me, the guy beside me, and whoever is driving, the van is empty.

Again, there's silence.

The van slows and turns right, then speeds up. Looking out the windshield, I notice we've turned onto an open stretch of road, leading out of any populated areas. The driver goes even faster, so fast I'm sure we're breaking the speed limit.

Panic rises again. This is not normal. I'm not going anywhere near a police station.

Tugging on the handcuffs, they make a rattling sound against the interior side of the van. The man beside me turns, arches one brow and smirks at me. The smirk is menacing, his eyes seem demonic. He's hiding a secret, and he's not telling me what that secret is. I swing my body around in order to touch him, but he slides back and out of my reach.

"Sit down, for your own safety," he orders.

I try and reach for him again. I need to know what he was looking at and where I'm going.

"Sit down!" He pulls a stun gun out of a holster behind him, warning me.

"Big man," I taunt. "Going to stun a seventeen-year-old girl who's handcuffed."

He smiles and looks forward out the front window.

Suddenly, I hear a massive bang. The van swerves from side to side, before it starts to drift down the edge of the road toward the ditch. I desperately hang on to the bar I'm handcuffed to. The van rolls, and the guy in the back gets thrown around like a rag doll. The van keeps rolling.

There's a sickening crunch, and popping sounds happening all around me as the momentum of the rolling causes my body to be flung around, while my head is continuously smashed against the bar and the metal of the van. I scream out in pain, as what feels like a blade tears through my leg.

The van eventually comes to a stop on its side. It's crumbled. Completely destroyed. And I'm handcuffed to it.

"Hey," I say to the guy who handcuffed me, but he's lying by my feet, completely unresponsive.

Blurry dots are clouding my vision, and I try to blink them away.

"Hey!" I yell with more urgency and move my foot to kick the guy in the shoulder. "HEY! HELP!" I bellow when I realize he's not in a good state. Looking forward, I try to see the driver, but he's not in his seat. The entire front of the van is completely destroyed. It's not even there anymore, it's been ripped off the vehicle.

More black spots darken my sight. Fogginess fills my brain. I'm hanging on, but just barely.

I can feel my body slipping from consciousness. I'm quickly being taken over by the impact of the car accident.

Closing my eyes, I still keep trying to shout. I can hear it myself, my voice is getting weaker.

Will anyone come looking for us?

Am I going to die here? Is that what's happening? Am I dying?

A bright light penetrates my eyelids, and forces me to open my eyes.

"Wear gloves," I hear a male say. I don't recognize the voice.

"I can handle a *pretty little* thing like her," another male responds. The lewd and creepy way he says 'pretty little' makes my skin crawl.

Fighting with my eyes, I try and open them so I can see who these people are.

"Come here, my cute little friend," the creepy guy says again. My body is swung around while something hot nips at my wrists. "I'm gonna have a lot of fun with this one."

The veil of darkness is winning. I'm losing it. Losing every ounce of control I have.

"I told you, she's not your toy. And wear gloves."

"Why do I have to wear gloves?"

"Because we're under instruction. He said we have to wear gloves, so wear your God damned gloves."

"This is stupid. Why should I wear gloves?"

"Because I heard him saying, she's got a gift."

"A gift? What the . . ."

Are you ready for more?

The Butterfly Effect Series book #2

THE CURSE

Keep reading for a special sneak peek

CHAPTER 1

Jude

With my phone in my hand, I pace the floor of my office. I stop every few steps and look down, waiting for *the* phone call to come.

"Where the hell is she?" I say aloud to no one.

Swallowing my anger, I run my hand through my hair, then down the back of my neck to squeeze the tense muscles. She's been gone for nearly two weeks, and no one knows what's happened to her.

Everyone I pay at the police department to keep me informed is failing miserably. I've called on every contact I have, and no one knows anything. It's like she's vanished.

The raid on my house was a damned ruse. It was orchestrated to get Lexi out and take her away from me. But I still have no idea who did this. One department is saying it's another department, and no one seems to know anything for sure.

Stopping in front of the desk, I swing my laptop around and play the security footage taken just before they took Lexi from me.

I watch as they come into my house, I watch how the men I paid to look after her froze and dropped to the floor instead of grabbing Alexa and hiding her in the safe room. They've all been fired, replaced with men I know will do exactly what they're supposed to do. Some are even mercenaries, hired for their comfort with extreme brute force.

Placing my phone on the desk, I flex my right hand and rub my bruised knuckles. Don, the guard at the door who let them enter my home, copped the worst from me. He let those animals inside my house. He let them take my girl without even questioning their fake credentials.

He had to be held responsible. He deserved what he got. Everyone knows what happens when you cross me.

I stretch my hand once more; the ache is a welcome. If I could, I'd go back and bludgeon his skull in again. But he's been disposed of, like the trash he is.

My eyes keep watching the screen, how they're handling my girl. They're careful not to touch her. They know. They have to know. They wouldn't go to all this trouble to get her if they didn't.

My head of security, Ronan, was with me when it all happened. He was remotely watching over the house, and the moment he saw it unfold and informed me, I left my meeting with the Sorrell family and took the jet straight back here. Hell, I even had the pilot put it down on the landing strip here, instead of at the hangar.

But we were six hours too late. Lexi was gone. Frank was beaten nearly to death, and most of my men were dumped in the middle of nowhere.

The van that took Lexi disappeared.

We can't find it, and we have no idea who has her.

Ronan's been searching and hacking into every security system he can to find her. I haven't slept since she's been gone. I'm on the very edge of losing my shit and about to start breaking down doors until I get the answers I need.

Ronan appears at my door, with his laptop in his hand. His eyes tell me I'm not going to like what he's found. She'd better be alive, or I'll find and torture every person who's been part of her death. Every person who's profited from, touched, or hurt her, *will die.*

"Ronan." I gesture for him to come into my office. "What have you got?"

He doesn't speak. He's usually the quiet type, the guy who gets things done and doesn't say much. I like him because he takes instruction well. He's been my right-hand man for as long as I've been in this business.

"I've found her." He types furiously on the screen, bringing up multiple images.

The one in the top left hand corner is of the van. Destroyed and crumpled. The front of the van is completely destroyed. It doesn't look like the driver could have survived the wreck.

"Who has her?" My eyes furiously search all the images on the screen.

Ronan is quiet.

Fury overtakes me.

Something inside me snaps. Ronan's silence is alarming and I'm ready to murder every fucker who's put their hands on her.

"Who has her?" I shout at Ronan.

"You're not going to like this . . ."

ALSO BY
Margaret McHeyzer

Dying Wish

I have three major loves in my life: my family, my best friend Becky, and ballet. Elijah Turner is quickly becoming the fourth.

He's been around as long as I can remember. But now he's much more than just the annoying guy at school.

My life was working out perfectly...until it got turned upside down.

Mistrust

I'm the popular girl at school.

The one everyone wants to be friends with.

I have the best boyfriend in the world, who's on the basketball team.

My parents adore me, and I absolutely love them. My sister and I have a great relationship too.

I'm a cheerleader, I have a high GPA and I'm liked even by the teachers.

It was a night which promised to be filled with love and fun until...something happened which changed everything.

Ugly

This is a dark YA/NA standalone, full-length novel. Contains violence and some explicit language

If I were dead, I wouldn't be able to see.

If I were dead, I wouldn't be able to feel.

If I were dead, he'd never raise his hand to me again.

If I were dead, his words wouldn't cut as deep as they do.

If I were dead, I'd be beautiful and I wouldn't be so...ugly.

I'm not dead...but I wish I was.

Chef Pierre

Holly Walker had everything she'd ever dreamed about – a happy marriage and being mum to beautiful brown-eyed Emma - until an accident nineteen months ago tore her world apart. Now she's a widow and single mother to a boisterous little 7-year-old girl, looking for a new start. Ready to take the next step, Holly has found herself a job as a maître d' at Table One, a once-acclaimed restaurant in the heart of Sydney. But one extremely arrogant Frenchman isn't going to be easy to work with...

Twenty years ago, Pierre LeRoux came to Australia, following the stunning Aussie girl he'd fallen in love with and married. He and his wife put their personal lives on hold, determined for Pierre to take Sydney's culinary society by storm. Just as his bright star was on the upswing, tragedy claimed the woman he was hopelessly in love with. He had been known as a Master Chef, but since his wife's death he has become known as a monster chef.

Can two broken people rebuild their lives and find happiness once more?

Smoke and Mirrors

Words can trick us.

Smoke obscures objects on the edge of our vision.

A mirror may reflect, but the eye sees what it wants.

A delicate scent can evoke another time and place, a memory from the past.

And a sentence can deceive you, even as you read it.

Grit

Recommended for 18 years and over

Alpha MC Prez Jaeger Dalton wants the land that was promised to him.

Sassy Phoenix Ward isn't about to let anyone take Freedom Run away from her.

He'll protect what's his.

She'll protect what's hers.

Jaeger is an arrogant ass, but he wants nothing more than Phoenix.

Phoenix is stubborn and headstrong, and she wants Jaeger out of her life.

Her father lost the family farm to gambling debts, but Jaeger isn't the only one who has a claim to the property.

Sometimes it's best to let things go.

But sometimes it's better to fight until the very end.

Yes, Master

My uncle abused me.

I was 10 years old when it started.

At 13 he told me I was no longer wanted because I had started to develop.

At 16 I was ready to kill him.

Today, I'm broken.

Today, I only breathe to survive.

My name's Sergeant Major Ryan Jenkins and today, I'm ready to tell you my story.

A Life Less Broken

On a day like any other, Allyn Sommers went off to work, not knowing that her life was about to be irrevocably and horrifically altered.

Three years later, Allyn is still a prisoner in her own home, held captive by harrowing fear. Broken and damaged, Allyn seeks help from someone that fate put in her path.

Dr. Dominic Shriver is a psychiatrist who's drawn to difficult cases. He must push past his own personal battles to help Allyn fight her monsters and nightmares.

Is Dr. Shriver the answer to her healing?

Can Allyn overcome being broken?

My Life for Yours

He's lived a life of high society and privilege; he chose to follow in his father's footsteps and become a Senator.

She's lived a life surrounded with underworld activity; she had no choice but to follow in her father's footsteps and take on the role of Mob Boss.

He wants to stamp out organized crime and can't be bought off.

She's the ruthless and tough Mob Boss where in her world all lines are blurred.

Their lives are completely different, two walks of life on the opposite ends of the law.

Being together doesn't make sense.

But being apart isn't an option

HiT Series Box Set

HiT 149

Anna Brookes is not your typical teenager. Her walls are not adorned with posters of boy bands or movie stars. Instead posters from Glock, Ruger, and Smith & Wesson grace her bedroom. Anna's mother abandoned her at birth, and her father, St. Cloud Police Chief Henry Brookes, taught her how to shoot and coached her to excellence. On Anna's fifteenth birthday, unwelcome guests join the celebration, and Anna's world is never the same. You'll meet the world's top assassin, 15, and follow her as she discovers the one hit she's not sure she can complete – Ben Pearson, the current St. Cloud Police Chief and a man with whom Anna has explosive sexual chemistry. Enter a world of intrigue, power, and treachery as Anna takes on old and new enemies, while falling in love with the one man with whom she can't have a relationship.

Anna Brookes in Training

Find out what happened to transform the fifteen-year-old Anna Brookes, the Girl with the Golden Aim, into the deadly assassin 15. After her father is killed and her home destroyed, orphan Anna Brookes finds herself homeless in Gulf Breeze, Florida. After she saves Lukas from a deadly attack, he takes her in and begins to train her in the assassin's craft. Learn how Lukas's unconventional training hones Anna's innate skills until she is as deadly as her mentor.

HiT for Freedom

Anna has decided to break off her steamy affair with Ben Pearson and leave St. Cloud, when she suspects a new threat to him. Katsu Vang is rich, powerful, and very interested in Anna. He's also evil to his core. Join Anna as she plays a dangerous game, getting closer to Katsu to discover his real purpose, while trying to keep Ben safe. Secrets are exposed and the future Anna hoped for is snatched from her grasp. Will Ben be able to save her?

HiT to Live

In the conclusion to the Anna Brookes saga, Ben and his sister Emily, with the help of Agent rescue Anna. For Anna and Ben, it's time to settle scores...and a time for the truth between them. From Sydney to the Philippines and back to the States, they take care of business. But a helpful stranger enters Anna's life, revealing more secrets...and a plan that Anna wants no part of. Can Anna and Ben shed their old lives and start a new one together, or will Anna's new-found family ruin their chances at a happily-ever-after?

Binary Law (co-authored)

Ellie Andrews has been receiving tutoring from Blake McCarthy for three years to help her improve her grades so she can get into one of the top universities to study law. And she's had a huge crush on him since she can remember.

Blake McCarthy is the geek at school that's had a crush on Ellie since the day he met her.

In their final tutoring session, Blake and Ellie finally become brave enough to take the leap of faith.

But, life has other plans and rips them apart. Six years later Blake and his best friends Ben and Billy have built a successful internet platform company 3BCubed, while Ellie is a successful and hardworking lawyer specializing in Corporate Law.

3BCubed is being threatened with a devastatingly large plagiarism case and when it lands on their lawyers desk, it's handed to the new Corporate Lawyer to handle and win.

Coincidence or perhaps fate will see Blake and Ellie pushed back together.

Binary Law will have Blake and Ellie propelled into a life that's a whirl wind of catastrophic events and situations where every emotion will be touched. Hurt will be experienced, happiness will be presented and love will be evident. But is that enough for Blake and Ellie be able to live out their own happily ever after?

Made in the USA
Columbia, SC
09 December 2017